SEEKING
VENGEANCE
(ATF ROMANTIC SUSPENSE)

BY
M.P. McDONALD

PROLOGUE

Sam Brennan tossed back his fifth shot, craving relief from the pain. As the heat of the alcohol burned into his belly, the numbing effects spread like a warm blanket. He poured another, held the glass at eye level and admired the flickering of the fireplace flames through the amber liquid. *Beautiful.* He downed the whiskey in one long gulp, hardly tasting the bite anymore.

A log popped and sent a shower of sparks swirling up the chimney. Whose idea was it to build a fire anyway? It was too damn cheery. Sam stepped back and flung the shot glass at the flames, feeling a measure of satisfaction at the explosion of glass against the back wall of the fireplace.

"Sam? Is everything okay?"

He turned to find Cynthia, his partner's wife, regarding him with concern. She dried a pink bowl as she spoke. A few hours ago, the bowl had held some kind of salad. The 'guests' had raved over it between offering their condolences. He was sick of everyone's concern. Sick of holding it together. Sick of being strong. "Everything is just peachy, don'tcha think?"

"Why don't you come back to our house tonight, Sam? Stay a few days until—"

"Until what? Until I get *over* this?" He stalked towards her but stopped short, as even in his drunken haze he recognized her suggestion was only an attempt to help. Her husband, Dave, had already offered their guest room. After five years at the same field office for the ATF, they were as close as brothers, but right now, the thought of being in Dave's home was unbearable.

Cynthia held her ground, shaking her head in sympathy. "No, that's not what I meant." She tossed the towel over her shoulder and held the bowl in front of her, hugging it against her stomach. Tears swam in her eyes and he felt like an ass. Cynthia and Dave had taken care of the details he couldn't face. "Dave's missed you and wants to be there for you."

Sam's undercover status had taken him out of the office for several months and he had missed the camaraderie too, but that was before. Before his world fell apart. "I know. Dave's a good guy." Sam's breath hitched as he stifled a sob. Good old Dave—the guy had everything and right now, Sam hated him. He hated that Dave had a beautiful wife and two adorable children. They were the perfect family. Guilt crept through his grief. It wasn't Dave's fault and he wouldn't wish his hell on anyone, let alone on his best friend, but at the same time, staying with Dave and Cynthia in their picture book home was the last place on earth Sam wanted to be tonight.

"I...I can't. Not tonight." Waves of pain crashed over him, drowning him in their intensity. His knees buckled and he sank to the floor.

"Sam!"

He felt Cynthia's arm drape over his shoulders as she eased down, kneeling beside him. "It's okay. Let it out. You'll feel better."

That was a lie. He'd never feel better. Not now, not *ever*. If crying would help, he'd cry buckets, but it wouldn't. Nothing would. He put his arm around Cynthia's waist, giving her an awkward hug. "I'm okay. Jus' too much to drink."

She pulled away, searching his eyes, but he averted his face. "Sam..."

He stood, pulling Cynthia to her feet as well. His years of working undercover had taught him that he could hide any emotion. His life had depended upon it. Now, he clung to the lessons learned, certain that if he let go and vented his grief, he'd lose his focus—lose the singular emotion that kept his heart beating.

Revenge

CHAPTER ONE

Gravel crunched under Sam Brennan's feet as he crossed the dusty lot. Sweat tickled a path down the back of his neck and he swiped it as he halted behind a row of parked motorcycles. Damn. No decals of black wings. The symbol of the Ravens biker gang had haunted his nightmares for the last year, but the tables had turned. He hunted them now.

He turned from the bikes and squinted at the bar. Raucous laughter spilled out of the open door. Early evening meant it would be relatively safe inside, but Sam adjusted the holster under his left arm and made sure his leather jacket hid the bulge. It was a given that he wouldn't be the only one packing. Sam took a deep breath and relaxed his shoulders, forcing himself to assume an easy rambling gait.

Pausing in the entrance, he blinked a few times until his eyes adjusted to the dim interior. The chatter diminished as the patrons noticed him, but after a few seconds, it ramped up to the previous volume. That was a good sign. Nobody recognized him. He'd counted on that. The thirty extra pounds he'd carried as part of his undercover persona, had melted away, leaving him back at his normal weight. His clean-shaven jaw completed the transformation. He bellied up to the bar and tossed a fifty on the scarred wood. "Bottle of Jack."

The bartender's eyes widened before he shrugged. "Sure." He dug a new bottle out from beneath the bar, grabbed a glass, and set both before Sam.

Sam gathered them, leaving the fifty as he settled at a table in the far corner where he could survey the rest of the room. He knew the generous tip would buy at least some measure of loyalty, but it would only last as long as the bottle lasted. That's fine. He didn't intend on staying long. He poured three fingers of whiskey in the glass and suppressed a grimace. Drinking hard liquor in the middle of the afternoon was something he didn't think he'd ever get used to. He'd become a master at nursing a drink, letting the inevitable drinking companions drain the contents of the bottle.

No sooner had he tipped the glass when his first 'guest' headed towards him. Sam pretended not to notice, keeping his eyes on the television. A ballgame played, but the sound was muted.

"This seat taken?"

Sam gave a backhanded wave, his eyes glued to the game. "Help yourself."

He pretended surprise when the man sat down. This guy was the scout. He'd dig for information and report back to some higher up. Sam had seen the routine dozens of times. Hell, he'd participated more times than he could count.

The man would make small talk first and then Sam would offer him a drink. Before long, a few more men would approach. They would size him up, prod him for information in the guise of being friendly. If they decided he had associations with the club, as they preferred to call themselves, he'd be okay, but if he didn't pass muster, it wouldn't go so well. If he was lucky, he'd be rolled for all his cash and that would be the end of it. Sam downed a second shot, clenching his jaw as the whiskey burned a trail down his throat. If he wasn't lucky, he'd be beaten or worse. He poured a third shot. Today was his lucky day. The hard metal nestled under his arm guaranteed that.

Sam didn't feel like playing the game today, and when the guy began his small talk, Sam glared at him. "What the hell do you think you're doing? Did I invite you to sit here?"

The young guy's mouth dropped open in surprise before he snapped it shut. He leaned forward, and Sam had to give him credit for having balls. "I don't ask no one permission to sit. I sit where I want, when I want."

A couple of zits dotted the guy's face and Sam wondered if the pup was even legal age to drink. Not that it mattered. At this kind of bar, the state didn't make the laws. The gangs made their own and enforced them with their own brand of justice. He shrugged. "Aw, hell. I don't care. Have a seat." Sam allowed a half-smile to play across his mouth. "Just having a bad day. Why don't you get yourself a glass and share a drink with me?"

The hostility eased in the young guy's eyes and he nodded. "Sounds good." He caught the bartender's attention and raised his chin. A moment later, a waitress dropped off a second glass.

Sam poured him a generous portion and lifted his own glass. "To better days."

The pup grinned and added his own toast. "To hot women!"

Sam laughed. "Can't argue with that." He tipped his drink, consuming only a minimum amount. The kid was all right. After refilling the glasses, Sam stuck out his hand. "I'm Sam."

The kid darted a look over his shoulder, and after a brief hesitation, clasped Sam's hand. "They call me Flea."

"Glad to meet you, Flea." He wondered how the kid had ended up with that nickname. It wasn't exactly terror inspiring, but he'd seen huge men called Rosie, so he wasn't about to question it.

An hour later, Sam had purchased another bottle and had a couple of new friends, Tuck and Scarecrow. They were a bit older than Flea, and treated the younger man like a kid brother.

Today, Sam was only looking to meet a few people so that he could ease into their trust. So far, his plan was working. They carried the second bottle of whiskey to the pool tables and had a few rounds. Sam made sure to lose most of the games, but won a couple, too.

He leaned on his pool cue, taking in the others. The patches on the back of their jackets identified them as the Miscreants—a minor biker gang, but one that had aspirations. If he could get in with them, it might be his ticket to finding Ray Howard, the enforcer in the Ravens. Sam had a bullet with that man's name on it. His window for using the bullet was closing because Sam had learned that an informant was already in custody, and with his testimony, Howard would be out of Sam's reach for years—possibly forever. Sam was sure any day, Howard would be arrested and then he'd go to trial. He couldn't let that happen. For a man like Howard, prison wasn't a punishment. He could operate just as well from the inside.

Feigning drunkenness wasn't difficult as he staggered out of the bar, Flea stumbling along beside him. He wondered if the kid was in any shape to drive. "Hey man, you want a ride?" Sam's bike was big enough for two.

Flea shook his head. "Naw, I only gotta go up the road." He fumbled with his keys, grinning when he dropped them and bent to fish them out of the weeds lining the path from the door to the parking lot. The action saved his life.

A motorcycle carrying two men roared through the parking lot like something out of a Mad Max movie. Sparks of fire shot from the muzzle of a gun aimed at Flea.

"Look out!" Sam leaped, pushing Flea behind the blocks of concrete dividers at the front of the parking lot. He covering him with his own body as gravel sprayed across them. Something stung his calf like a thousand yellow jackets and he grunted. When Flea tried to get up, Sam put a hand on the back of the other man's head, holding him still. "Keep your fool head down." He reached into his jacket for his gun.

Glass shattered, but he couldn't tell if it was from the bar windows or from vehicles in the lot. He dared a peek over the block and saw the bike come around for another pass. Sam squeezed off a few shots, hoping the sudden swerve of the bike meant he'd done some damage. A second later, he had to duck when the passenger let loose another spray of bullets. He swore as shards of concrete stung his neck and was thankful he wore his leather coat despite the heat. He felt like a sitting duck and wasn't sure if the answering fire from within the bar was a good thing or not. While it wasn't aimed at them, bullets pinged off the blocks and burrowed into the ground all around them. He hissed at sudden burning across his back up near his shoulder.

The element of surprise lost, the bike roared away, leaving the parking lot eerily silent except for the tinkle of glass hitting the ground. After a few moments, the bikers inside poured out. Tuck and Scarecrow leaped down the steps and rushed to their side. Others followed, shouting obscenities at the retreating tail light of the motorcycle.

Sam holstered his gun and grit his teeth as he levered up to sit on the concrete block closest to him. His leg throbbed, but the pain across his shoulders kept him from leaning forward to inspect the damage. He sat, hands gripping his knees and tried not to pass out.

"Flea? Man, you okay?"

Sam glanced up as Tuck bent down beside Flea. Had the kid been shot?

Flea's hands dropped from covering his head to the grass, and he pushed to his feet. "Shit. Yeah, I think so. Man…What the hell was that about?"

Scarecrow scrutinized Sam before turning to Flea. "Those were Ravens. I think they're still gunning for you, Flea."

Sam wanted to ask about that, but sirens wailed in the distance. Soon, the cops would be crawling all over the place and that was the last thing he wanted. He needed to get to his bike and get the hell out of Dodge. Unable to suppress a grunt, he stood and took a few hobbling steps before his vision started tunneling. *Damn it.* He blinked and shook his head.

"Sam? Were you hit?" Tuck's hand gripped Sam's right elbow, steadying him.

"Nothing major, just a couple of grazes I think. Might have just been gravel."

"Let me see."

Tuck tried to steer him back to the concrete block, but Sam shook him off. "No, gotta get…going. Police will be here…soon."

"Sam, you're bleeding." Flea wavered in Sam's vision.

"I gotta go." The police would blow everything. He stumbled towards his bike, but seconds later, Tuck and Flea were beside him.

Tuck put an arm around Sam's waist. "Lean on me. We'll get you out of here."

Grateful for the help, Sam pointed out his bike and pulled his keys out of his pocket as they neared it.

Tuck took the keys from him. "I'll drive." Sam nodded, and climbed onto the higher backseat. The sirens were closing in. Tuck said something to Flea and shouted something to someone back at the bar, but Sam couldn't focus on what they were saying.

A moment later, Tuck straddled the bike. "Hold on."

Sam clutched the side handles, groaning when he had to raise his left leg onto the peg. In spite of the warm temperature, he began shaking and clenched his jaw to keep his teeth from chattering. He had no idea where they were going, he just held on and prayed he wouldn't fall off.

Dimly, he sensed another bike beside them and guessed it was Flea. The guy had been drunk as a skunk just a few minutes ago and Sam credited adrenaline for sobering up the kid so quickly.

Tuck seemed to be taking every corner at full speed and it was all Sam could do to keep his balance. The rest of the ride passed in a blur of neon lights and a few minutes later, just the occasional blur of a porch light from a house. The road narrowed as they left town, and walls of corn, darker than the sky, closed in on them from each side.

The bike slowed and turned onto a gravel road. Sam had to bite his lip to keep from crying out as they hit a pothole. A dark shape loomed ahead of them. A garage. Whose garage? Tuck drove behind the garage, stopping the bike out of sight of the road. The headlight from Flea's bike swept over them as he turned the corner and parked alongside them.

Tuck leaned down and took Sam's right hand, draping it over his own shoulders. His other arm went around Sam's waist. "Come on, I got ya."

Sam nodded and put his right foot on the ground. Getting the left one over the seat was tricky, but with a grunt, he completed the maneuver.

Flea came up on Sam's left. "I'm going to run up to the door and let Molly know what's going on." He took off at a sprint.

"Jeez, that kid has way too much energy," Tuck muttered, and if Sam could have mustered up a laugh, he would have, but he could only nod in agreement.

Sam wondered who Molly was and what she'd think of them showing up like this.

It took them five minutes to navigate the side yard in the dark, the outside light didn't come on until they hit the porch.

Hushed but heated voices came from the doorway as the trio climbed the steps.

"Come on, Molly. You can help him. You know what will happen if he goes to the hospital. Everything will get reported."

"I could lose my license over this, Johnny."

Sam lifted his head, focusing on the slim form huddled in the doorway, her arms wrapped around her body as though warding off a chill. "Excuse me, ma'am, if you have some gauze and tape, I can fix it up in no time and be on my way. "

It had been awhile since he'd applied a field dressing, but he was pretty sure he could do it. At least for the leg. The back would be harder, but he'd manage. Somehow.

The woman turned to him, one hand sweeping a riot of dark curls behind her shoulder. After taking a head-to-toe appraisal, her gaze lingered on his left leg and how Sam favored it. Finally, she sighed and turned with a half-hearted beckoning gesture. "Bring him in."

* * *

"Don't let the door slam; Kelsie's sleeping." Molly Flynn led the way down the hall and turned into the kitchen. What had her brother gotten involved in this time? When would he learn that bikers were nothing but trouble? It was a lesson she had learned well and she just wished Johnny could learn from her mistakes instead of creating a whole slew of his own. She cringed at the noise the men made as they followed behind her, their boots loud enough to wake the dead as they clattered on the hardwood floor. The injured guy grunted and she heard Johnny whisper an apology.

She blew a few strands of hair out of her face as she gave thanks that Kelsie slept like a rock. Molly pulled a chair out from the table and angled it. "Put him here, and Johnny, you need to grab a dishrag and clean up any blood on the floor."

"Okay, but then I have to go take Tuck back to the bar to get his bike."

On her way to retrieve some items she needed, Molly spun back to Johnny. "*What?* You're leaving?"

Johnny wrung out a rag and shot her a guilty look. "I'll be back as soon as I can."

Molly marched up to her brother, flicking a worried glance at the man in the chair as she passed. The guy listed to the right and she hoped he wouldn't topple off the seat. She snagged the back of Johnny's collar. "Come here. I need to speak with you."

"But—"

"*Now!*" She led the way to the hallway and gave him a little shove. "Are you *crazy*?"

Johnny's eyes widened. "What do you mean?"

"You arrive on my doorstep late at night with some biker who was shot up in some kind of…of…*brawl*. You drop him off in my kitchen as if I run a twenty-four hour clinic and then think you can just *leave?* What am *I* supposed to do with him?"

At his blank look, she poked his shoulder with a stiffened pointer finger. "I have a six year-old daughter, in case you've forgotten."

He shrugged. "So?"

"*So?* That's all you can say? You bring a strange man in here and put us at risk? What were you *thinking*?"

"I was thinking you're almost a doctor, and if anyone could help him, it'd be you." He stared at the floor and shuffled his feet a few times but then raised his gaze, his eyes pleading. "He saved my life, Molls. What was I supposed to do?"

"He saved your life?"

Johnny twisted the rag in his hands and nodded. "A couple of Ravens showed up as we were leaving the bar. Sam yelled out a warning, and I looked up, but froze. He knocked me to the ground."

That did put a different spin on the situation and added a sense of obligation. She hated obligations. "Ravens?"

Nodding, Johnny added, "But don't worry. Snake wasn't one of them."

Molly shot a glance back into the kitchen before closing the few feet between her and Johnny. "What have I told you about mentioning that name in this house?"

Dipping his head, Johnny nodded then shrugged. "I know. You hate it, but Kelsie's not even awake, so what's the big deal?"

"The big deal is that while the name is fitting, I'll grant you that, I won't have you buying into his mystique load of crap and that's what that name does. It makes him seem dangerous and evil. But really, he's just a greedy, power hungry...jerk," Molly finished, her hands fisted at her sides as she leaned towards Johnny. She had an endless mental list of foul names for the man, but she refused to even voice them out of stubbornness. Jerk was perfect and wouldn't feed anyone's ego. Blowing out a breath, she took a step back and smoothed a hand over her hair as she sought to get back to the topic at hand. With a vague gesture towards the kitchen, she asked, "And his name is Sam?" At least it wasn't some silly nickname.

"Yeah, and he seemed like a nice enough guy before. Bought drinks all night long."

"He's after something. You know that, right?" There was a fishy smell about the situation, but then again, that was par for the course where her brother was concerned. She turned from him. "Get the blood cleaned up, take Tuck back, and then return here pronto. This isn't a hospital and one year of med school doesn't make me a doctor. I'm just a paramedic."

"You're the best paramedic I know." He gave her one of his trademark grins and she rolled her eyes.

Johnny reached out and tousled her hair in the way he'd done since he was a kid. He knew she hated when he did that. It annoyed her how it called attention to the unruly curls that she fought to keep under control, but it was also his way of reminding her that they were siblings. She swatted his hand. "Knock it off. Besides, I'm the *only* paramedic you know."

His grin only widened. "I'll be back in in a few hours, Molls. I swear it." The screen door slammed as he left.

Molly shook her head and went to bathroom medicine cabinet and juggled peroxide, bandages, and tape down the hall to the kitchen. Setting the supplies beside the paper towels and clean rags on the table, she tried to think if she'd need anything else. She grabbed an old bath towel from the linen closet as an afterthought, tossing it on the floor just in front of Sam's foot. His eyes followed her movements but every few seconds he closed them and a muscle in his jaw tensed. His color didn't look so good and she wondered just how badly he was hurt. Johnny had made it sound like the guy just had a few scratches.

"I'm sorry to cause you trouble, ma'am." His voice was deep with a hint of roughness.

Molly tore off strips of tape and hung them on the edge of the table so they'd be easy to reach when she needed a piece. "I'll be honest. I'm not thrilled about my brother dropping you off here. I'll do what I can, but I'm not a doctor, just a paramedic."

"I appreciate it."

She moved to the sink, filled a bowl with warm water and returned, setting it on the table beside his chair. The back of his leather jacket had a gash angling from just below the shoulder blade area, ending at the right shoulder. Great. He could have a spinal injury and here she was treating him with tape and paper towels at her kitchen table. "You should go to a hospital. You know that, don't you?"

Sam lifted his head, his eyes hard. "That's not an option."

He moved as if to stand, and she rested a hand on his shoulder, pressing down lightly. "Sit. I said I'd do what I could, but I'd be remiss if I didn't advise you that you'd be better off with a real doctor."

He gasped, grimacing, and she snatched her hand away. "Sorry. I hope I didn't hurt you."

He nodded, but his face was pale against his dark hair. "No. It's okay."

"Listen, maybe I'm getting ahead of myself. Let's take a look and see what we're dealing with, okay? If it's beyond my scope, I'll let you know."

His eyes met hers. Not quite green, but not quite hazel, they wavered for a moment as he let out a deep breath. "Yeah. Okay."

"First, I'm Molly—Johnny's sister."

"Johnny?" His brow knit in confusion.

"You probably know him as Flea." She shook her head and couldn't hold back the sarcasm. "His buddies in that motorcycle," she made air quotes with her fingers, "*club*, gave him that stupid nickname."

"Ah. Yeah. I figured it wasn't his given name."

Molly chuckled. "No, his mother was smarter than that. Not much, but a little." She retrieved other items she'd need out of a cupboard, including a Dutch oven to act as a bucket when she cleaned his leg, as well as a pitcher she usually used for making lemonade.

"I take it you don't share a mother?"

"No. He's my half-brother. He said your name is Sam."
She set the Dutch oven on the floor and straightened, putting her hands on her hips. Do you have a last name, Sam?"

He averted his face. "I do."

She waited but when he wasn't forthcoming, she shrugged. "Whatever. Let's get this over with. You need to take off your jacket."

He unzipped it but had trouble getting it off. She grasped the right cuff and he pulled his arm as she eased the leather over his shoulder and slid it down his arm. Molly stilled at the sight of a gun in a holster strapped over his shoulder. "I don't allow weapons in my home."

She expected defiance, but Sam merely unbuckled the holster and set it on the table. "I don't much like them either. You can hang onto it if you want."

Molly stared at the weapon, then picked it up by the holster straps and put it on top of her refrigerator for the time being. Turning back to Sam, she said, "Before we go any further, do you have any more surprises in store for me?"

Wearily, he shook his head. "No, ma'am."

He didn't sound like a biker and she cocked her head, studying him. So he was a polite one. If it was one thing she'd learned over the years, it was that bikers came from all walks of life. She even knew a few doctors who put on the leather and tried to be tough on the weekend. Thinking of leather, she glanced at the jacket still in her hand. The lining was saturated with blood. No wonder he looked so shocky. She tossed it in a corner. "I think that's beyond repair."

He didn't act too upset about the loss, and that made her wonder. Most motorcycle guys she knew would rather give up an arm than their jacket. "Before I start working, I want you to drink something. You need fluids." She raised an eyebrow at him as she moved to the refrigerator. "Non-alcoholic fluids," she clarified.

She had milk, water, juice and a couple of diet sodas. The juice would have to do. As she reached for it, she noticed the bottle of children's electrolyte solution in the back. She'd bought it when Kelsie had been sick with a stomach bug the month before. Perfect.

She poured some in a large glass and handed it to him and hid a smile when he gagged on the first swallow.

"What is this crap?" He wiped his mouth with the back of his hand and glared at her.

So much for Mr. Politeness. "It's what you get when you're dehydrated and need fluid replacement. It's not like I have an IV in my medicine cabinet. Quit acting like a baby and drink it."

"I'm not dehydrated. I've been drinking all afternoon."

She thought she'd detected the faint odor of whiskey on his breath, but Johnny's had been a lot stronger. "That's *why* you're dehydrated—that, and blood loss."

She rifled through her junk drawer for an old pair of bandage scissors, ignoring his muttering about how she was trying to poison him. Finding the scissors, she moved to his side again. "I need to cut your t-shirt off, unless you're able to get it off yourself."

He glanced at his blood-soaked shirt and shook his head. "It's not like I can ever wear this again. Go for it."

Molly made quick work of the shirt and tried to hide her dismay at the deep gouge across his back. She wasn't an expert, but she had seen a few bullet wounds on the job before. One end of the gouge was deeper and had a large bruise already radiating from the impact. "I can clean this up and throw some butterfly tape on it, but I still think you need to see a doctor, get some x-rays, antibiotics and stitches." She cleaned the wound, dabbing the edges with the clean rags.

He sucked in a breath between his teeth as she worked, but otherwise kept silent. She did the same, working quickly as she smeared antibiotic ointment along the wound, laid clean wet gauze over it and secured it with tightly crossed strips of tape. Over that, she set a large dry dressing, taping that loosely over the other.

Next, she went to work on his leg, tearing his jeans up the seam to his knee to get a better look at the injury. The bullet had passed through the muscle of his calf, leaving an exit wound on the inside of his leg through the thickest part of the muscle. Concerned about damaged nerves and broken bones, she removed his boot and sock, and assessed the limb. There was no deformity and he was able to wiggle his toes when asked although he grunted in pain. The pedal pulse was strong—that was a good sign. She ran her hands down the sides of his leg to his ankle, feeling for any irregularities, then had him rotate his foot.

His hands tightened on the seat of the chair.

"Are you okay?"

He nodded, but when she released his foot, he blew out a deep breath and perspiration dotted his face.

Molly frowned. "Sorry. I just want to make sure you have full range of motion."

"Yeah. I know." He cleared his throat. "No apology necessary. I'm good."

Blood loss was moderate compared to his back. That was a relief. Fluids would help, but they wouldn't replace a transfusion if he'd been hemorrhaging. Molly set the boot aside for the moment, but hoped it would be salvageable. Her closet was full of shoes, but she didn't own any that were his size. A snicker bubbled out at the image of this rough and tumble biker in a pair of her strappy sandals. His eyebrow arched at her giggle, but he didn't comment.

Unable to get a good angle to work on his leg, Molly dragged another chair out and helped him rest his leg on it. She poured a pitcher of clean tap water over the wound, irrigating it until the water cascading into the Dutch oven on the floor beneath had only a faint pink tint. The edges of the wounds were clean, not ragged, so she just added the ointment and a loose dressing. "When was the last time you had a tetanus shot?"

"Last summer." He held up his hand, palm out, and she saw a faint pink scar. "I cut myself." His quick answer satisfied her that he was telling the truth. Most people had no idea.

"Good." Pointing to his glass of electrolyte solution, she said, "Drink up. Johnny should be back soon."

He grimaced but took another sip. When he tried to hold back another gag, she took pity on him, and dumped the solution in the sink. Moving to the fridge, she pulled out the orange juice and refilled his glass with it instead. It occurred to her that she hadn't offered anything for pain. All she had was ibuprofen, but it would at least take the edge off a little. She found the bottle on the counter where she'd left it after taking a few this afternoon, and shook out three, handing them to him with the juice. "Here."

"Thanks." His mouth quirked into a ghost of a smile. He downed the pills and must have been thirsty despite his earlier claims of not being dehydrated because he tipped the glass, draining it. Afterwards, he rested his head against the seat back and closed his eyes.

Molly put the ibuprofen away and turned back to find Sam dozing. Deciding sleep was the best thing for him at the moment, she let him rest and set about cleaning the mess in her kitchen. Gathering up the bloody rags, she disposed of them then dumped the Dutch oven and used the towel to mop up any splatters on the floor.

The last thing she did was rinse the boot, then stuffed the towel she'd used on the floor into the boot, attempting to soak up as much water as she could. She hoped the leather wouldn't shrink, but if she hadn't rinsed the boot, it would have shrunk anyway from the wet blood.

Holding the boot in her hand, she thought for a minute. If she put something in it to mimic a foot, it might not shrink too badly. Five minutes later, she found an unopened bag of brown sugar and smiled. She wrapped it in another layer of plastic wrap in case the bag broke and then crammed it in the boot, molding the sugar into the approximate shape of a foot.

She glanced at the clock when she finished. Johnny should have been back by now. Damn him. It was already two in the morning. In less than five hours, she'd have to wake Kelsie, get her off to school, and after that, run a bunch of errands.

Exhausted, she sank onto a chair and scrubbed her hands through her hair. Sam still slept, but he'd be stiff if he stayed like that much longer. The medic in her took over, wondering if there was something more she should do. He probably needed to be on antibiotics, but if he refused to go to the hospital, there wasn't much she could do.

She rested her head on her crossed arms on the table. Where in the world was Johnny? The last thing she wanted was to wait for her brother to come and retrieve his friend. She turned her head against her arm and tried to stifle a yawn, but lost the battle. When she opened her eyes, she found Sam watching her, but his gaze wasn't threatening, just tired.

He blinked, and she envied his thick eyelashes. Why did guys always get them? "I can wait for your brother on the front porch. I don't want to put you through any more trouble than I already have."

Molly flushed. It wasn't his fault her brother never kept his word. "No, that's okay." She straightened, wincing at the kink in her back. "Besides, I'm pretty sure Johnny isn't coming back. At least, not tonight."

"Well, I'll head out on my own then. I think Tuck gave me back my keys." He patted his front pockets, and then fished into the right one, pulling out a key ring. He sat forward and eased his leg off the chair, giving a small groan when his bare foot hit the floor. He glanced at the spot she had first tossed his boot, before turning to her with a questioning look.

"Oh yeah. I had to clean it. It's going to take a while to dry."

"How am I going to ride my bike without a boot?" He waved a hand at his foot.

She almost laughed at his befuddled expression. "I guess you can't. I put it out on the front steps where the sun will hit it first thing. It should dry in no time tomorrow."

He stood and hobbled to the hallway.

Molly followed behind him, puzzled. "Where are you going?"

Sam turned. "Out to the porch. I'll have to put the boot on or it'll never fit me again."

She rolled her eyes. "You can't sleep on my couch with a wet boot on your foot. I won't allow it."

His eyebrows rose. "You'll let me sleep on your couch?" The hope in his eyes transformed his face and lent him a boyish charm.

"What else can I do? I have to get to bed, and you're stuck here."

He watched her for a few seconds, undefinable emotions flitting through his eyes, then he nodded and said, "Thank you." The boyishness replaced by weariness.

She made up a bed on the sofa while he cleaned up in the bathroom. Who was this guy? He wasn't like the usual friends Johnny hung out with. No matter how many times she warned him about the bikers, he just didn't listen, but she remembered the fascination they held for her at one time. It seemed like a lifetime ago. Whatever appeal they had held for her was long gone and she couldn't even recall what it was that she found so intriguing. She guessed it was the bad boy image. She smiled and shook out a blanket, letting it float down on to the sofa. Johnny couldn't fathom that Molly would rather spend an evening playing Candyland with her daughter than flying down the road on the back of a Harley.

Her job took her away from home two nights a week as it was. Tucking the sheet under the cushions, she sighed. Kelsie had to stay at the sitter down the street on those days and even though she knew she should feel fortunate that she had a good one so close, she hated leaving her. The older woman liked the company and filled the role of grandmother for the little girl who never got to meet her own grandma.

Sam came out of the bathroom wearing the old sweatpants she'd given him. Johnny had left the pair after some other adventure. They were too short for Sam, but better than his torn, bloody jeans. She didn't have a shirt that would fit him and was embarrassed to feel warmth creep up her face as he crossed the living room.

His broad shoulders tapered to a narrow waist, his skin golden in the dim light. He appeared lean and fit. It had been ages since she'd been with a man, but she saw plenty of well-built guys at the firehouse, so why did she feel the flutter in her stomach as Sam limped towards her? She tore her gaze away and tossed the pillow from the armchair to the end of the couch. The flutter was most likely a result of fatigue.

"There you go. It's not the Hyatt, but I hope it's not too lumpy," she joked to cover her confusion. Luckily, he didn't seem to notice.

"I'm sure it's fine. I'm so tired, I think I could sleep on a bed of knives." He looked like he tried to grin, but lines of pain etched between his eyes as he eased down to sit on the edge of the sofa.

"Okay, well, I'll leave you alone now. If you need anything, just holler. I'm a light sleeper, and my daughter can sleep through a tornado, so don't worry."

He put his feet up and tugged the covers to his waist with a sigh. "Good night. I'll be fine. Get some sleep while you still can. I'm sure the first school bell rings awfully early."

She paused as she reached for the light switch. The few guys she'd dated since having Kelsie never voiced concern about how early she had to wake to get her daughter off to school. "Good night."

Before she left the room, she heard his breathing settle into a deep even rhythm.

CHAPTER TWO

The clatter of dishes awoke Sam with a start. Sunlight streamed into his eyes when he opened them and he winced before squinting at his surroundings. The throb in his leg and the tight ache across his back announced the previous night's events, but he barely remembered lying down. A sharp stab of pain between his eyes reminded him that he'd also had more to drink the day before than he was used to—nothing like a hangover to go with bullet wounds.

He heard Molly speaking in the kitchen, but couldn't make out what she was saying. Even without hearing the words, he recognized the sing-song cadence. By the time a sweet little voice replied, he'd steeled his emotions and was able to ignore the infectious giggle that floated from the kitchen.

It took him several minutes to lever to a sitting position, and he had to pause and gather his strength before standing. His head felt heavy and his eyes burned. He vowed to never drink whiskey again. The bathroom was just down the hall; he could see the door from where he stood, but it felt like miles as he limped to it. After finishing his business, he washed his hands and splashed his face, hoping to clear some of the fog in his brain. A tentative knock sounded on the door.

"Sam?"

He turned off the faucet and reached for a towel, swiping the water off his face and chest as he opened the door. "Yeah?"

"I found an extra toothbrush. Kelsie got a couple the last time she went to the dentist."

Sam took the child-sized toothbrush. "Thanks."

She nodded. "No problem. Sorry it's so small."

He tried to smile—tried not to remember a similar toothbrush in his own bathroom. "It's okay." A chuckle slipped out. "I might have to brush my teeth one-by-one with it, but I'll manage."

Molly reached behind her head and tightened her ponytail, unmindful of a few wisps that curled along her face. "Great. So, I have to take Kelsie to school. Normally she takes the bus, but she's taking her biggest stuffed dog in for show and tell." She dropped her hands and hiked her purse up her shoulder.

Sam gripped the toothbrush, feeling like a fool. He should have woken up sooner and gotten out of her hair. "I'll just brush real quick, and be right out."

She tilted her head, confusion crossing her face, then her eyes widened and she held a hand up. "Oh, no. I'm not trying to rush you. You don't have to take off yet. You need to eat, and later, I'll need to change those bandages."

"You trust me to stay here while you're gone?" He wasn't sure whether to be grateful or angry. Didn't she realize the possible consequences? For all she knew, he could be a murderer. Hell, it was his *plan* to become one.

"Are you going to rob me?"

"Hell no, I'm not going to rob you, but—"

"Then shut up and say thank you." She glared at him for second before shaking her head.

"Thank you."

She lifted her chin and gave a short nod. "You're welcome." Moving a few steps down the hall, she stopped in front of the next door, a smile curving her profile as her face softened. "Kelsie hon, you can only take Tiger with you. Put the other animals back on your bed."

He heard Kelsie call good-bye to the other stuffed animals and his heart clenched. A second later, a tiny little girl with curls a shade lighter than her mother's hopped into the hallway, her face obscured by a gigantic stuffed blue dog.

"Come on, Kel, we have to hurry." Molly put her hand on her daughter's head and glanced back at Sam.

He cleared his throat and waved the toothbrush. "Thanks again."

She nodded, not quite smiling.

After brushing his teeth, he wandered out to the kitchen looking for something to drink. He'd hoped his leg and back would loosen up once he was up moving around, but the wounds seemed to be competing for his attention with each trying to outdo the other.

In the fridge, he found the orange juice and didn't think she'd mind if he helped himself. It tasted tart after brushing his teeth, but he welcomed the icy cold as it slid over his tongue. When he finished, he left the glass in the sink. It had been almost twenty-four hours since he'd eaten, and he knew he should, but the idea of food repulsed him.

He went back to the living room, intending to fold his bedding, but a wave of dizziness swept over him, forcing him to sit on the couch instead. A little while later, the dizziness passed, but he felt no inclination to move. What he needed was a couple more ibuprofen, but didn't want to rifle her cabinets looking for it. How far was the school anyway? She'd been gone almost an hour. He rubbed his forehead, trying to ease the ache between his eyes. Sighing, he rested his head against the back of the sofa.

* * *

Molly opened the back door; Sam's boot in one hand, a bag of items she'd picked up from the store, in the other. The boot wasn't completely dry, but she didn't want the sun bleaching it either.

She set the bag on the table. "Sam?" There was no answer and apprehension crawled through her. What if he had robbed her and left? Not that she had much worth stealing—just a few pieces of jewelry from her mother, as well as a computer. She didn't think Sam could carry a computer and drive his motorcycle at the same time, but the jewelry was portable. The boot in her hand caught her attention. Wait a minute. He couldn't go—not with just one boot.

Still holding it, she walked into the living room and found him sitting on the sofa, head back, eyes closed. For a second, she admired the broad expanse of chest and his square jaw, darkened by a day's growth of beard, but then noticed the flush on his cheeks. She set the boot by the front door and crossed the room, pressing a hand against his forehead. Hot. *Crap.*

He started awake, his eyes glazed. "Hey."

"Hey yourself. You're burning up."

He shook his head. "I'm freezing." He shivered and reached for the blanket sitting beside him.

"I have to get stuff together to change your dressings. Don't lie down yet."

"Okay."

She wasn't sure he knew what he was agreeing to, but she hurried to gather what she needed as quickly as possible before he fell back to sleep. What would she do if he had an infection? She should have reported a gunshot wound but she hadn't. If she lost her job, what would she do? How would she take care of her daughter?

"Damn it all to hell," she muttered as she carried the supplies out to the living room. When she saw Johnny again, she was going to rip him a new one.

"Sam, take these, then sit forward so I can get to your back." She handed him three ibuprofen, and a glass of water.

Dutifully, he took the pills and leaned forward. She cleaned the wound, applied more ointment, and re-bandaged it. As she applied tape, she noticed a scar lower on his back just above the waistline of the sweatpants. It wasn't large, but she recognized it for what it was. No wonder he wasn't too concerned about this injury. Compared to the healed wound, this one was a mere scratch.

At least two times in his life, this guy had been shot. That wasn't exactly the kind of man she wanted around her daughter. Even if the target of last night's shooting was her brother, Sam had been there. Most people knew to avoid rough bars and seedy neighborhoods.

Finished, she patted the couch. "Go ahead and sit back if you want. I need you to bring your foot up on the coffee table so I can check your leg." She felt a twinge of sympathy when he winced as his back touched the sofa.

"Is my boot dry? I should probably get going."

Molly paused while unwrapping his leg and glanced at him. He watched her with eyes bright with fever. There was no way he'd make it a mile on a bike. "Sorry, not yet. Besides, I guess you'll need some clothes to wear. If you can wait a bit longer, I'll run to the department store over in Franklin and pick up what you need." The wound was clean and dry, so she wrapped it with a clean strip of gauze. "You should keep that elevated as much as possible."

He sighed. "Don't take this wrong, because I appreciate what you've done for me, but I need to get the hell out of here as soon as I can."

"Believe me, no offense taken because I feel the same way. The sooner you're gone, the better." Did he think she was trying to keep him here on purpose? She slammed the roll of bandages back in the first aid kit. "If I thought you were capable of handling that huge bike of yours, I'd drag you out there myself and give you a big wave as you roared away; but tell me, Sam, what if you pass out while driving? What if you misjudge a curve and take out an innocent mother or father, or God-forbid, a whole family?" She tucked the box under her arm and glared at him. "You may not care about things like family, but other people do and I won't risk that."

A flash of anguish shot through his eyes before he closed them briefly. She studied him, curious about the flash. It was almost as if she had slapped him, but the expression vanished so quickly, she wondered if she'd imagined it.

Now, he regarded her with a mask of indifference. "Fine. I feel like shit, so I guess you're right."

"I'm always right." She tried to lighten the remark with a wink, but he'd turned his head away. Guilt jabbed her but she ignored it and headed for the bathroom where she stashed the first-aid box in the closet. There was no reason for guilt. Whatever caused the pain she'd seen, it was none of her doing.

Taking a moment away from him, she threw in a load of laundry, tidied up Kelsie's room and then headed to the kitchen. The more she tried to forget about the man in her living room, the more he intruded on her thoughts. She stopped at the sink and cast a look around the kitchen. It didn't look like Sam had eaten at all. Other than a glass with a few drops of orange juice in it, the kitchen looked exactly the same as when she had left.

The guy needed to eat something if he was going to get any strength back. To further that goal, she dropped two slices of bread in the toaster, poured another glass of juice, and when the toast popped, buttered it and placed it on a plate. With a jar of grape jelly tucked under her arm, she carried the items into the living room and set them on the coffee table.

Sam held out a hundred dollar bill.

Molly stared at it, puzzled. "What's that for?"

"For the clothes."

She plucked the bill from his fingers. "Okay, but I'm only going to the nearest discount store. I'm pretty sure this is more than I need."

"It's the smallest I have. Sorry."

Crap. Had the guy robbed a bank before heading to the bar? Johnny had said Sam had bought drinks all night long.

"Why don't you get something for your dinner with the change? It's the least I can do."

Every time she wanted to pound him into the image of a rough biker, he said or did something that altered how she saw him. "Thank you. Kelsie loves chicken fingers, so I guess I'll get some of those."

He'd taken a few bites of the toast but now lay back. In seconds, he was asleep.

She decided to leave his breakfast there in case he woke and was hungry.

* * *

Sam shifted on the couch, unable to find a comfortable position. Molly had left a while ago and he felt like a stray dog that she was stuck with. They should have let him drive his own bike. He'd have headed to his motel. It was a forty-mile drive, but he was sure he could have made it. With the damn fever, he was in worse shape now. At least in his rented room, he'd be in a bed. Not that he didn't appreciate Molly's help, he just hated causing trouble.

In the confusion of the shooting and aftermath, he'd almost forgotten Tuck's comment to Johnny about how the shooters had been aiming for the kid. Why would the Ravens be trying to kill the guy? And would their attempts at revenge eventually extend to Molly and her daughter?

He'd have to find Johnny and question him. If he could get the kid to talk, it might be key to Sam getting his own revenge. The Ravens had to be stopped.

Sitting on the edge of the couch, he drank some juice and still thirsty when he finished it, decided to get some water. His head pounded with each hobbling step as he crossed the living room towards the kitchen, but he decided to make a detour to the bathroom first.

After washing his hands, he wondered if the medicine cabinet held the bottle of ibuprofen. It had only been a few hours, but he knew he could take one more and be okay. A twinge of guilt washed over him as he opened the mirror. Normally, he'd have no compunction about snooping. It was his job, but not in this situation. Avoiding the small box of tampons, he couldn't help hesitating when he saw the circle of a birth control pill dispenser. Was Molly in a relationship? Was some guy going to walk in and get the wrong idea?

He shook his head. It wasn't any of his business, and he'd be gone soon. On the second shelf, he found the pain medication beside a bottle of children's acetaminophen. After shaking a pill out, he went to the kitchen and filled a glass with water, washing the medication down.

His leg throbbed by the time he made it back to the couch and he cursed his weakness as he shivered. His teeth chattered and he tightened the blanket. Soon, he fell into a restless sleep.

Disjointed images of fire filled his dreams. In them, he rushed around in the flames always searching. Panic and desperation consumed him, and he shouted.

* * *

"Sam! Wake up!" Molly shook his shoulder, alarmed at the heat radiating from his skin.

His eyes snapped wide with panic. "I can't find him. Help me!" He sat straight up, turning his head as though looking for something.

Molly crouched in front of him, trying to cut into his field of vision, but he seemed to look right through her. "Who? Who are you looking for, Sam?"

"Sean. I gotta find him. But the fire and smoke…" He coughed and waved a hand in front of his face. "It's so hot. *Sean?*"

The raw pain in his voice tore at her, but when he attempted to stand, she held his shoulders, pressing down and urged him to stay seated. "It's okay. You're only dreaming." She had to repeat it several times, before he finally focused on her. He blinked as if trying to place her face before she saw recognition. "Are you okay now?"

He rubbed his face, scrubbing at his eyes. "Yeah. Sorry."

"No need to apologize, but I don't think there's any chance of you leaving today."

"I shouldn't have let your brother bring me here. I didn't realize where we were going."

She sighed. "It's not your fault. My brother is always screwing up." Molly winced at her choice of words and the way Sam flinched at them. "I didn't mean that like how it sounded. I truly don't blame you for this and I'm grateful to you for saving my brother's life." She sat beside him on the edge of the sofa and gave a slight shrug. "It's always something with him, but…he's my brother."

"Why are the Ravens targeting him?" Sam slanted a look at her.

Surprised at his bluntness, she stared at him for a long moment before answering, "I don't know, and even if I did, I don't think it's any of your business." His eyes narrowed, but she cut him off as he opened his mouth. "Don't tell me it's your business because you threw yourself over Johnny. That was your choice. Nobody asked you to."

"I think getting caught in the crossfire damn well did make it my business, but aside from that, I was asking because I thought I could help."

"How could *you* help?" It was on the tip of her tongue to add why he would offer. What was in it for him?

Sam stood, wincing as he straightened. "I've had some dealings with them before." He hobbled down the hall seeming to feel right at home as he entered the bathroom.

Molly remained on the edge of the sofa for a few moments, wondering if Sam had a clue what he was dealing with. She knew first-hand how cruel biker gangs could be, but if Sam was like other guys she had tried to warn, he would brush off her warnings. She had learned to stop trying. Sam had walked off in the middle of the conversation anyway, so slapping her palms on her thighs, she muttered, "Well, I guess that's the end of the discussion."

She rose and went to the kitchen to retrieve the bag of clothing she'd bought for Sam. It had felt odd buying clothes for a man. Not knowing what he'd like, she bought a couple of t-shirts and a button down shirt along with packages of socks, boxers and a pair of jeans. She intended to carry them out to the living room, but as she rounded the corner she ran face first into his chest.

He gripped her shoulders, steadying her as she stumbled backwards. "Whoa. Excuse me."

Her nose smarted, but his scent still lingered and distracted her from the pain. She tasted a slight saltiness on her lips from where they had brushed his skin. She stared at him for a moment before thrusting the stack of packages at him. "Here are some of the things I got you."

Sam took them, but he looked puzzled. "Are you okay?"

"No. I mean, yeah. Everything's fine." Flustered, but working to hide it, her reply sounded cold even to her own ears. Not used to feeling unsure of herself, she reacted with anger. "Why wouldn't I be?"

"I thought maybe you hurt your nose." He pointed towards her face with the packages.

"It smarted a little, but it's no big deal." She resisted the urge to step closer. Just because she hadn't been alone with a man for a couple of years didn't mean she could act like a fool around Sam. He didn't even appear to notice her, at least, not in the way men usually noticed a woman. Pride stinging more than her nose, she turned away, calling over her shoulder as she returned to the kitchen, "If you want to shower, go ahead. I can re-do the bandages when you come out."

Thankful when she heard the bathroom door shut, she gripped the edge of the counter and closed her eyes as she attempted to erase his scent from her mind and his taste from her lips.

* * *

Sam limped back to the bathroom, his mind a jumble of confusion. What had just happened out there? He could still feel the heat of her breath on his chest and he glanced down, half-expecting to see the imprint of her lips. When he'd steadied her, his hands had skimmed her arms and the feel of her skin, so soft and warm, lingered on his palms. Closing his eyes, he recalled the sun-warmed mint and vanilla scent of her hair and had to resist the urge to seek her out and repeat the encounter. Maybe it was just his fever causing the reaction, but he had felt a stirring he hadn't felt in over a year and the bolt of lust shocked him. He forced the demons of guilt to chase the reaction back to a dark corner of his mind. He had no right to think of her like that. She had generously taken care of him and had trusted him to stay in her home. Women like her didn't go for hardened bikers and even though he was only playing a role, in her eyes, that's what he was—just another biker friend of her brother's.

Sam stripped off his clothes and stepped into the shower. The pulsing stream of water eased some of the ache from his shoulders and other parts of his body. Her shampoo sat on a corner caddy, and he smiled. Yep. Vanilla-mint.

The shower revived him, restoring some of his energy, so he took advantage of it and, after the shower. He unfolded the jeans, but debated pulling them on. Molly said she'd replace the soggy bandages, and he doubted the leg of the jeans would roll high enough to allow her to get to the wound. He could just stay in his boxers. The devilish thought made him chuckle as he slipped the sweats he'd worn earlier over his legs. He shook out a t-shirt and draped it over his shoulder as he went in search of Molly.

He found her in the kitchen sitting at the table cutting potatoes into wedges. Before speaking, he watched her work. Her back was to him, her slim neck revealed by the ponytail. Wisps of hair drew his attention and the impulse to push them out of the way and replace them with his lips swept over him. He fought it off and knocked on the doorjamb. "Molly?" It was the first time he'd said her name aloud and he liked the feel of it rolling off his tongue.

She started, the knife rattling as she dropped it on the table. "Done already?" Her eyes flicked to him, lingering on his jaw, so he knew she noticed the difference, but she didn't comment on it. He'd hoped the clean shaven look would make him appear less sinister.

Instead, she asked about the clothes "They didn't fit?"

Sam shook his head. "I didn't try them yet…well, except for the boxers." He felt his face heat, and wanted to roll his eyes at himself. Why was he reacting like a teenager? The woman had bought the damn underwear for him after all. "I just thought it would be easier to put a new bandage on my leg with the sweatpants on."

Molly stood, and he could have sworn her cheeks were pinker than they'd been a few seconds ago. She swept the pile of cut potatoes into a bowl and set them by the stove. "Makes sense. Let me just get these into the oven. I have to get Kelsie from school soon and then the craziness begins." She threw him a grin, her eyes dancing.

Damn, she was beautiful. The thought blindsided him like a meteor out of a clear blue sky.

"Uh, no problem." He licked his suddenly dry lips and then remembered what he had come to ask her. "Do you have a bag or something I can put my dirty clothes in?"

"Yeah." Without another word, she took a plastic grocery bag from under the sink and brought it to him. "Will this work?"

"Perfect." He took it, wanting to linger, but he had no excuse to stand and stare, so he returned to the bathroom and put it back in order, stashing his bag of clothes by his boots near the front door.

Molly had cleared the table and had the bandages ready by the time he entered the kitchen. It only took a few minutes and she pronounced his wounds healing nicely.

Finished, Sam changed into the new jeans and t-shirt, feeling normal for the first time since he'd arrived.

* * *

Molly stood outside the school waiting with other parents for their children. She hoped Kelsie had given the teacher her note that she was being picked up today. The chicken fingers needed to go in the oven and the potatoes needed turning. She should have waited to start them until after picking up Kelsie, but the weather was so nice, she liked to eat early and let Kelsie play outside until bath time. She was so glad there were only a few more days of school. Summer was always easier without the morning rush and the homework—although admittedly, at Kelsie's age, homework consisted of one worksheet or reading. The reading part was fine as it was part of their bedtime routine anyway.

The bell rang, and Molly scanned the faces, but it wasn't until almost all the other kids had left before Kelsie ambled out with Tiger clutched in her arms. The impatience Molly had felt drained away when Kelsie spotted her and grinned, her eyes lighting up. "Mommy!" She broke into a run, but with the stuffed animal in her arms, she couldn't see where she was going and tripped at an uneven spot on the pavement.

"Kelsie!" Molly rushed forward to help her. Her daughter scrambled up, her bottom lip quivering as she clutched a scraped knee.

"It's bleeding!" Big, fat tears rolled down Kelsie's face and dripped onto the sidewalk.

"Aw, sweetie. It's not so bad." Molly bent to examine the leg. The skinned knee was smudged with blood, but nothing an adhesive bandage couldn't cure. She pulled Kelsie in for a hug. "Shhhh...hey, guess what?"

Kelsie sniffled. "What?"

"Tiger saved you. He's a hero!" Molly reached over and tugged the giant dog towards them. "He broke your fall. You would have bumped your nose on the sidewalk if not for him." She gave the dog a little shake.

Kelsie's eyes grew big. "He *is* a hero!"

"Yep. And when we get home, I'll fix your knee up in no time, okay?" She glanced at her watch and stood, taking Kelsie's backpack and Tiger in one hand, and Kelsie's hand in the other. "I have another surprise. We're having your favorite dinner of all time."

"Spaghetti?"

Molly laughed. "No, your *other* favorite. Chicken fingers!"

"Yum!" She tugged Molly's hand. "Come on, you're being a slowpoke, Mommy."

After helping Kelsie with her seat belt, Molly slid behind the wheel and sighed. Of course there had to be a whole line of buses waiting to exit the drive and they had the misfortune of being behind a bus all the way home, slowing them even more. The potatoes were sure to be burnt and the chicken fingers still frozen. She drummed her fingers on the wheel, only half-listening as Kelsie chattered in the backseat.

Almost an hour after she'd left, she pulled in her driveway. She rushed Kelsie up the steps into the house. "Hurry up, hon. I have to get the chicken fingers in the oven. You go put Tiger away and then I'll fix up your leg, okay?"

Kelsie nodded and skipped through the kitchen. Molly followed her in, sniffing the air. Nothing was burning, and she could have sworn that adding to the potato scent was the aroma of baking chicken fingers. She set Kelsie's backpack on a chair and peeked into the oven. "What in the world?" The chicken fingers looked almost done, and the potatoes had been turned, the wedges a golden brown and nearly ready to come out.

Molly walked into the living room, about to ask about the dinner, but stopped short. Kelsie sat on the coffee table, her sundress hiked up as she pointed out her owie to Sam. "I got a boo-boo like you. My mommy's gonna fix it, but guess what? Tiger saved me, and we're gonna have chicken fingers!"

Sam nodded as he regarded Kelsie's injured knee and the stuffed animal. "Yeah, that's some dog you have there." He reached out and chucked Tiger's muzzle.

"Yep!" Kelsie jumped off the table, the toe of her shoe colliding with Sam's injured leg. He jerked, but said nothing, his lips tight.

"Kelsie!" Molly moved into the living room. "Say you're sorry."

"What?"

"You just hurt Mr...Mr. Sam's owie with your foot. You have to be more careful."

Kelsie looked from Sam to Molly, her lip pushing out. "I didn't mean to."

"I know, hon, but you need to apologize."

Sam waved his hand. "It's fine. It was an accident and I had my leg in the way."

"See, Mommy?"

Molly sighed. "Yes, I see, but you still need to apologize."

Her eyes brimming, Kelsie turned to Sam. "I'm sorry. I didn't mean to kick your owie."

The corner of Sam's eyes crinkled as he tilted his head and reached out, his fingers brushing over Kelsie's hair before he pulled his hand back. He cleared his throat. "I know you didn't."

The tears dried up instantly and Kelsie beamed first at Sam and then turned her smile on Molly.

Molly watched the exchange, wondering at the softness in Sam's expression, but Kelsie ran over to her and hugged her waist before she could process it fully. Pushing Kelsie's hair out of her eyes, Molly bent and kissed her forehead. "Go wash up for dinner and put Tiger in your room like I told you." She gave her a nudge towards the hall. When the little girl was in her room, she turned to Sam. "Sorry."

"Don't worry about it. I can handle a six-year old's kick." His mouth quirked, but sorrow shadowed his eyes.

"She can be pretty headstrong." Molly crossed her arms. "Thank you for managing dinner for me. I appreciate it."

Sam shrugged, wincing at the motion. "Not a big deal. I owe you."

"No. Johnny owes me, but regardless, I appreciate the help. It was very thoughtful of you." Molly noticed a flush staining Sam's cheeks and bit back a smile. The guy was uncomfortable with praise. "So, do you feel up to eating with us tonight?"

"Sure." Sam stood, his limp a bit more pronounced as he made his way to the kitchen.

She wondered if she should take a look at his leg to see if any damage had been done, but Kelsie ran out of the bathroom holding a box of bandage strips. "Oh, hon. I almost forgot. Let me fix you up.

"

CHAPTER THREE

Feeling awkward, Sam leaned against the counter while Molly cleaned Kelsie's knee, and he felt a catch in his throat when she bent to kiss the scrape before putting the bandage on it. He remembered the days when a kiss could make everything all better. Looking for something to take his mind off the past, he scanned the kitchen and spotted the pot-holders. The chicken and potatoes were probably done.

"Want me to get the stuff out of the oven?" Without waiting for an answer, he grabbed the oven mitts, and opened the oven door.

"Sure. That would be great. I'm just going to nuke some corn. It'll only take a few minutes."

Molly opened the can of vegetables, poured them into a bowl and popped it in the microwave while Sam deposited three chicken fingers and a half-dozen wedges on Kelsie's plate. "How many do you want? Four? Five?" He held the baking sheet in one hand, a spatula in the other as he waited for Molly's reply.

The microwave beeped, and Molly glanced at him. "Five. I'm starving. And lots of wedges."

Sam grinned. "You got it."

He took the same for himself then returned the pan to the top of the stove. "You want something to drink? I can pour us something."

Molly laughed as she pulled the corn from the microwave. "This feels so odd. I'm not used to having help, but that would be great. Kelsie gets milk, but I'll have some of the lemonade in the pitcher. Help yourself to whatever looks good."

Sam pulled two glasses and a child's plastic cup from the cabinet. It did feel odd, yet also comfortable. He chose orange juice again, poured Molly her request and filled Kelsie's cup with milk. He set his and Molly's drinks at their places, and turned to get the milk.

Molly had already grabbed it, but struggled to carry the corn, ketchup and the cup. He did a quick hobble towards her, reaching for the ketchup and milk. "After you." He gestured to her chair.

Molly slanted him a smile. "What a gentleman."

Sam felt warmth build in his chest. "Not really. I'm just hungry." He put the milk in front of Kelsie. "There ya go, punkin."

The endearment slipped out before he could check it and guilt stole over him. It had been awhile since he'd used that tone of voice and he couldn't deny that it felt good, as though everything was okay. But, it wasn't okay and it wouldn't be until he finished his mission. He stabbed a piece of chicken with his fork and ate it, doing his best to tune out Kelsie's chatter and Molly's laughter.

"Mr. Sam?"

"Sam?"

He jerked his head up, suddenly aware that they were both looking at him as though waiting for a reply. "I'm sorry. I didn't catch the question."

Molly's head tilted and she regarded him with a curious expression. "It's nothing. Kelsie just wondered where you learned to cook."

Embarrassed, Sam pasted on a smile. "All I did was stick it in the oven." He pointed his fork at Molly. "Your mom did the hard stuff."

Kelsie dipped a piece of chicken into a pile of ketchup and poked her finger at the ketchup covering the tip of the food. "Sometimes Mommy burns it." She licked her finger.

Startled, Sam couldn't help laughing. "Is that so?" He grinned at Molly.

Molly covered her mouth and nose with her hands, but her laughter bubbled out. "Kelsie's right. I'm not the greatest chef in the world." She lowered her hands and she shook her head. "Hon, you're not supposed to tell people that." The crinkle at the corners of her eyes gave her away.

"But it's the truth." Kelsie's brown eyes became saucers. "You always said to tell the truth."

She turned the look on Sam, and he was sure the ice around his heart melted just a little bit. *Damn it*. He had to get out of here tomorrow. He averted his eyes and ate a potato wedge.

Molly voice sounded puzzled as she answered Kelsie. "Yes, you're right. I do say that."

There was an uneasy quiet, broken only by the sound of silverware clinking against the dishes.

"I'm full, Mommy. Can I go out and play with Gavin?"

"Sure, hon. Put your plate in the sink first."

The little girl skipped out the back door, and Sam stood, carrying his plate to the sink, and rinsed it.

"You don't have to do that." Molly followed him to the sink, her own plate in hand.

Sam glanced over his shoulder, ignoring her comment and taking her plate from her, adding it to his own as he rinsed it. "I can clean this up if you have something else you want to do."

Molly quirked an eyebrow. "Seriously? You don't mind doing dishes?" Her lips curved.

He gave a half-shrug. "What else have I got to do?" The truth was, he was tired of sitting on the couch and felt guilty for causing extra work. He soaped up a sponge and scrubbed the plates, running them under the faucet to rinse them.

"Okay. I'll take you up on the offer, but I'm going to clear the table first."

"Suit yourself."

A few minutes later, she left a small stack of dishes beside the sink and wiped off the table before heading outside.

Sam made short work of the rest of the dishes, saving the baking sheets for last. A few times, he heard Molly call to Kelsie. The little girl's laughter floated back to him, a slightly deeper laugh mingling with hers. A boyish belly laugh.

He pressed his fingers against the edge of the sink until the hand clutching his heart released its grip. When would it get easier? He grabbed a clean sponge and wet it before he scrubbed out his pain on Molly's counter tops.

"Hey?" Molly touched his forearm. "You realize that the gray is the actual granite, right? It doesn't come off."

Sam couldn't look at her. "Sorry."

Molly glanced at the counter, then took the sponge from him and tossed it in the sink. "Sam, I realize I don't know you very well, but what's going on? I don't have to be a paramedic to see that you're hurting."

Sam stared at the speckled gray stone but words and emotions tangled in his throat.

"What were you doing at that bar? You don't belong there any more than Kelsie would."

Had his undercover skills always been so bad? Had everyone seen through his cover? Deep inside, he'd known that somehow it had been his fault. Now, Molly's observations confirmed it. "You're right. I didn't belong there." He laughed, the sound harsh and bitter. "I don't belong anywhere."

He wiped his hands on his jeans and yanked a chair out, half-falling as he sat. It was the most that he'd been on his bad leg, but he almost welcomed the pain as a distraction.

* * *

"Tell me about it." Molly leaned her back against the counter, arms crossed, waiting. She knew his wounds bothered him, but that wasn't the reason for his pain. It went deeper. He was quiet for so long, she thought he would ignore her, but he closed his eyes as though gathering his thoughts.

He finally focused on her. "For the last twelve years, I've worked for the ATF."

Surprise mingled with satisfaction that she'd been right. He wasn't a thug like most of Johnny's friends.

"A year ago, I killed my son."

Caught off guard by the statement, Molly could only gape at him. She managed to close her mouth after a moment. Sam could not have killed his son. Not intentionally. She recalled the way his expression softened every time he looked at Kelsie. He was no child killer. "I don't believe you."

He broke eye contact, a faraway look settling on his face. "I'd been working undercover and infiltrated the motorcycle gang called the Ravens. I finally had enough evidence to prove that they were running arms and drugs. They had several legit businesses they used as fronts and to launder the money, but I obtained some documents and ledgers. I had a contact, and I was followed one day when I went to meet her."

Molly shifted, swallowing hard as she glanced out the window and spotted Kelsie and Gavin engrossed in hunting for grasshoppers. Good. That would keep them occupied for a while. This wasn't a conversation her daughter should overhear. She slid onto the chair opposite Sam.

"Nothing happened that day. I didn't know I'd been followed, but Sherry, my contact, was run off the road on her way back to the office."

"Oh my God!"

Sam waved a hand. "She was okay, and we attributed it to a drunk. It wasn't until later we found out it was intentional." He rubbed his eyes, bridging his nose before continuing, "I was deep undercover—hadn't seen my son for over a month. He was staying with my mom."

Where was the boy's own mother? At Molly's questioning look, Sam said, "His mother was someone I knew from high school. At our ten year class reunion, we had a…a thing." He blushed and if the subject hadn't been so serious, Molly would have smiled and teased him. "She didn't want to be married to someone in law enforcement. Later, I found out why."

He shrugged, wincing slightly. "After Sean was born, she tried to be a mom, but was more in love with meth." He made a face. "See, my job would have been a major cramp in her style. Eventually, she agreed to grant me full custody."

Molly had seen the nasty effects of meth and it wasn't pretty. "Wise decision."

Sam's eyes blazed and he slapped his hand down on the table. "*No!* It was the worst damn decision she ever made. If she'd been a *decent* mother, she would have kept Sean. She would have kept him away from *me*." He lurched to his feet and limped across the kitchen, stopping at the back door. He leaned a forearm on the doorway and stared out into the yard. "It would have stopped him from being killed because of my damn pride."

A muscle in his jaw flexed and she felt dread churn her stomach. She was sure it couldn't be his fault, but Molly didn't want to ask—didn't want to know what had happened. As a mother, she protected herself by saying bad things only happened to strangers. Sam was no longer a stranger and she was afraid to find out how Sean had died, as if the knowledge would rip apart the protective barrier she had built around her own daughter. But Molly couldn't let it drop—not when Sam blamed himself. Swallowing hard, she asked, "What happened to Sean?"

It seemed to take effort for Sam to tear his gaze from the children playing. When he did, she caught her breath at the depth of pain in his eyes.

"The enforcer of the Ravens had my mother's house torched. She and Sean were trapped inside."

She gasped, tears springing to her eyes. "I'm so sorry, Sam." There was nothing more she could say. It wasn't his fault, but she could see how he might blame himself.

If he noticed the tears, he didn't give any indication, instead, he stabbed a hand through his hair, making it stick out in a dozen different directions. "My mother died trying to save Sean. Their bodies were found by the back door."

Molly stood, needing to comfort him somehow. She moved behind him and tentatively touched his shoulder.

His muscles quivered and when she tried to catch his eye, he averted his face. "Sam. Look at me."

He ignored her.

"Listen, Sam, I missed the part where *you* killed your son. The way it sounds to me, some thug was responsible, not you."

He shook her hand off and brushed past her. She only had a brief glimpse, but the setting sun reflected a tear streak on his face an instant before he lifted his arm and swiped his face along his shoulder.

She followed him as he moved into the living room. "Hey, you didn't answer me." He might hate her for pushing, but he had to say it aloud. He needed to acknowledge that it wasn't his fault. "Look, I barely know you, but I've seen the way you are around Kelsie, there's no way you're capable of knowingly doing anything that would have jeopardized your own son."

He shot her a bitter smile as he began folding the sheets and blankets on the sofa. "You're right; you don't know me. You have no idea what I'm capable of."

Molly crossed her arms. "You don't scare me." The dark look he directed at her made her a liar.

He stalked towards her and it was all she could do to hold her ground. "You must have some notion that I'm this honorable ATF agent, but you'd be dead wrong. When Sean died, I decided that playing by the rules was for suckers." He reached for her and wrapped his hand around the back of her neck, pulling her close. "For example, an honorable agent would never do this."

Molly's heart thundered in her ears as she fought the impulse to twist out of his grip. She had to prove to him that he wasn't bad. His fingers worked into the hair at the nape. She couldn't suppress the shiver that rippled down her back, but she lifted her chin in defiance.

His gaze lowered to her mouth, and her heart sped up, only it wasn't fear this time. When he leaned towards her, she raised on tiptoe to meet him.

She expected a rough kiss, but his lips brushed hers teasingly. Closing her eyes, her other senses came alive. His scent filled the air she breathed. Shaving cream, soap and a light muskiness. It was completely male and all encompassing. She pulled his head down with one hand, wanting more. The kiss, begun in anger and defiance, grew bolder as she touched his chest. It felt warm and firm beneath her fingers, his heart thudding against her palm.

The kiss deepened as he pulled her against his body and tilted his head. When he began nibbling a path down her throat, she thought her knees would buckle.

"Mommy!"

The screen door slammed and Molly shoved away from Sam. He turned from her without a word and stalked to the front window.

She smoothed her hair away from her face and faced the kitchen doorway just as Kelsie burst through.

"Hey, hon—what are you hollering about?"

"I caught a lightning bug!" She had her hands cupped and lifted them in front of Molly's face.

"Wow! You must be faster than a greased pig at a sausage factory to catch one of those by yourself."

Kelsie beamed. "I am." She skipped towards the window. "Want to see, Mr. Sam?"

Sam turned and when Kelsie opened her hands to show him, the bug flew out.

"Oh no! He's getting away," Kelsie squealed.

His hand shot out, catching the escapee. "Here you go, sweetheart." He gently put his closed hand over Kelsie's and Molly was struck by the contrast of his strong tanned hands and Kelsie's small pudgy ones.

"Thanks!" Kelsie's tongue stuck out of the corner of her mouth as she concentrated on not squishing her prisoner. "Can I keep him for a pet?"

Molly crossed her arms as she shook her head. "Hon, don't you think his family will miss him?"

Kelsie's lip jutted out like she was going to protest, but after a moment, she nodded. "Yeah. His mommy would miss him, just like you'd miss me."

Molly winced at Sam's stricken look. She ushered Kelsie towards the kitchen, throwing a glance over her shoulder. He once again had his back to the room. "That's right, sweetie. Why don't we go return your little guy to the backyard and tomorrow night, you can visit him again. How does that sound?"

"Sure, Mommy."

Molly ruffled Kelsie's curls, thankful for her daughter's easygoing nature.

Kelsie beamed up at her. "I named him Buggy."

Only half-listening, Molly said, "That's a perfect name." She held the door as Kelsie ran out to the middle of the yard and consulted with Gavin, who was still pouncing on hapless lightning bugs. A few seconds later, after some whispered message into her hands, Kelsie released Buggy back to the wild.

When the boy ran to catch it, Kelsie yelled at him. Molly leaned against the doorframe, a smile curving her lips at her daughter's protectiveness of her Buggy. She couldn't imagine life without her sweet little girl and swallowed a lump in her throat at what Sam must have gone through—was still going through. For a brief moment, when he had pulled her close, she had felt a spark of fear, but thinking back, his grip had been firm but not forceful. It was a world of difference from other experiences she had endured. The taste of his kiss lingered on her lips.

The twilight deepened and Molly pushed away from the doorway, taking a few steps into the yard. She squatted beside her daughter who was watching a lightning bug glow in a tuft of grass. She put her arm around her shoulders, drawing her up. "Bath time, hon."

* * *

Sam sat on the sofa and worked on his boot. The leather was stiff and he swore as he bent it back and forth. He should have asked Molly to pick up some cheap boots, just something to get him on his bike and out of here. There was no denying it. If he stayed any longer, he'd end up doing something he'd regret. His chest seemed to burn where her hand had rested. Sam sucked in a breath and yanked at the leather, hoping that if he concentrated on the boot hard enough, he could forget the way the defiance in her eyes had flamed into something more— a passion and fire that threatened to consume him. He swallowed hard. And her body. She'd melted against him and he'd felt every curve. It felt so right, but it couldn't be. He slammed the door on the possibilities. There wasn't time for complications.

Guilt stole over him as he heard Kelsie chattering in the bathroom. Every time he spoke to her, he thought of his son. Sean would be eight now, but when he'd died, he was just a little older than Kelsie. It wasn't the little girl's fault, but every giggle and innocent question felt like someone ripping the scab off a wound. He wasn't ready to be around kids, that much was certain.

With a muttered curse, he bent the toe of the boot back and forth a few times to loosen it. The effort caused pain to pulsate through his shoulders and he lost his grip on the boot. It thudded to the floor.

"Sam?" Molly hurried into the room. Her skin glowed from the heat and steam of the bathroom.

He ached to caress it. "Sorry. Just dropped my boot." The pain in his back forgotten, he tried not to stare at the damp spot on the front of her shirt. It caused the fabric to cling in all the right places.

Something of what he felt must have shown on his face, because her cheeks turned rosy and she backed down the hallway before she ducked into the bathroom again. "Hurry up and brush, Kels. You're already up past your bedtime."

For the next twenty minutes, Sam sat in the living room. He pretended it was because his back and leg hurt too much to move, but the soft murmurs and giggles coming from Kelsie's room sounded like the sweetest music to his ears. Despite the ache centered in his chest, he relished the memories that rushed to the front of his brain. Making his son breakfast, supervising his baths and best of all, tucking him in at night. On evenings like this, Sean would play outside until the last ray of sunlight had been swallowed by the horizon, and then he'd fight sleep. It was like he was so afraid he'd miss something that Sam would have to corral the boy and throw him over a shoulder kicking and hollering. By the time they reached Sean's room, the child would be belly laughing and pounding on Sam's back.

Sam would toss him like a sack of potatoes on the bed. Then he'd tuck him in. He closed his eyes, remembering the scent of his son's hair. It was a sweet mixture of little boy sweat, sunshine and fresh air.

His breath caught as his throat swelled. It hurt so damn bad. He bent his head and tried to swallow the knot of pain. Tears sprang to his eyes and he blinked them away. He was a grown man, for Pete's sake.

The sofa cushion dipped and he felt Molly sit beside him. Embarrassed, he refused to look at her. He hadn't cried since the funeral. Now, in the space of a few hours, he'd been reduced to tears twice for no reason.

Molly' rested her hand on his forearm, stroking gently. She didn't speak, just touched. Her fingers, feather-light, seared a path on his skin. He held his breath when her hand dropped to his leg. She applied more pressure, running her hand up the outside of his thigh.

Grief and desire collided, merging into a supernova of emotion. Sam stood and pulled her up against him. She offered no resistance as he covered her mouth with his own. His hands roamed her back as they kissed. He shivered as her fingers ran through his hair. She tasted so good, and he couldn't get enough. He soaked up her touch and taste like parched earth in a summer storm. He slid a hand beneath her shirt and thrilled at the shudder that swept her as he cupped her breast. Her skin was smooth and warm. She offered her neck to him as he trailed kisses to her collarbone.

"Wait. Not here."

Sam dragged his mouth away. "What?"

"My room. Not here." Molly tugged his hand and led him down the hall.

He admired the fit of her jeans as she led the way. Inside, she shut the door and pressed him against it with a kiss as she worked at the buttons of his shirt. Surprised, but turned on more than he thought possible, he allowed her to do what she wished. He groaned when she licked his chest and grinned at the impish gleam in her eyes.

He decided two could play this game as he reached for the hem of her polo and tugged it over her head, tossing it to the side. Her arms draped around his neck, and he slid his hands over her shoulders and down her back as he claimed another kiss. He needed her skin against his, and he sought the clasp on her bra, making short work of it, easing the straps down her arms. She pressed against his chest and he groaned, wanting to savor every new sensation but needing even more.

He ached to taste and touch every inch of her. As though reading his mind, she backed up until her legs hit the edge of the bed and then she lay back. The impish smile was gone, instead her eyes burned into his as she undid the snap on her jeans. Sam swallowed. Hard.

* * *

Molly gripped the edge of the bathroom vanity. What had she done? Her nerves still tingled. The few times she'd been with men since Kelsie had been born had been brief, disappointing encounters. One had been a fellow paramedic that Molly had been attracted to for months. When they'd gone out, she'd been too eager. When she saw him a few days later, she'd been devastated when he'd treated her no differently than before. She'd been so wrapped up in her crush on the guy that she'd been blinded to the fact that he didn't feel the same way about her. She was just an easy lay to him. Embarrassed at her behavior, she'd only dated one other man since then. That time, she'd let him pursue her, and after several months, they slept together. It had ended in a disaster of awkwardness. It had been worse before Kelsie's birth, but she rarely allowed those memories to surface. There was no comparison to what she and Sam had done, with the act that had resulted in Kelsie's birth. Technically it might have been the same thing, but emotionally, they were polar opposites. Unwilling to spoil tonight's magic, Molly pushed the painful memories from her past back into the vault in her mind where she kept them under lock and key.

After that, she swore off men, sure that there must be something wrong with her. Sex wasn't all that it was cracked up to be, and she didn't miss it. Or so she'd believed, until now.

Sam had taken things slow, allowing her desire to go from simmering to a full boil before he'd entered her. He kept her on the edge until she wanted to explode—and then she *did* explode. At least, it felt like it. Molly blushed at her reflection in the mirror. The feeling had been like nothing she'd ever experienced before. What must he think of her? Covering her face with her hands, she felt heat climb her cheeks as she remembered how she had moaned and whimpered without shame at the time, but now? Now, she wanted to die of embarrassment.

The second Sam finished, Molly had rolled off the bed and escaped to the bathroom, mumbling about cleaning up. She opened the medicine cabinet and grabbed her birth control pills, popping out the one for today and downing it with a handful of water. She splashed some more water on her face, brushed her teeth and combed her hair. She glanced at the back of the door, relieved to see her sleep shirt hanging there. It wasn't much, just a comfy old t-shirt, but she didn't think she could parade in front of Sam nude—even if he had already seen all of her.

Now what should she do? She couldn't very well banish him to the couch after what they'd shared. Molly hugged the t-shirt to her chest. Had he really shared himself with her or had she just been a convenient emotional outlet? Did she have feelings for him beyond that of being grateful that he'd saved Johnny? It wasn't just gratitude, she knew that, but it might have been that mixed with an incredible attraction. Balling the shirt up, she buried her face in it. What had she done?

Molly pulled the shirt over her head and took a deep breath before opening the door. She needn't have worried about covering herself because Sam dozed, his dark hair brushing over his forehead, giving him a boyish look. Padding to the side of the bed, Molly tried to slip under the covers without disturbing him.

His bare chest rose and fell with each breath and his pulse beat steadily in his neck. She'd seen him sleeping before on the sofa, but this was different. He wasn't burning with fever or grimacing in pain now. Instead, he was dead to the world, completely relaxed. Molly smiled and longed to run her fingers over his chest and explore him as he'd done her. She'd been too shy to indulge her desires and she wondered if there would be a second opportunity. His wounds had healed enough for him to ride his bike and she knew he'd be leaving tomorrow. Now might be her only chance.

She hesitated when he moved, but as he settled again, she traced her fingers over his ribs. Like silk over steel. The sheet covered him to his hips, and she admired the way his torso tapered and felt her face heat as she contemplated reaching beneath the sheet, but she couldn't do it. She wasn't bold enough. Not yet. She let her hand rest just above his belly button and scooted closer. With a sigh, she closed her eyes and felt herself drifting, instinctively seeking his warmth as she edged towards sleep.

CHAPTER FOUR

Pounding on the door startled Sam out of a deep sleep. Disoriented, he shot from the bed, blinking in the darkness. Where the hell was he? It took a moment to get his bearings, and Molly's gasp from the bed helped him become oriented. Her eyes, wide with terror, reflected the dim moonlight filtering in the window. She jumped out of bed dressed in an oversized white t-shirt. Any other time he might have admired how it draped over her curves but now wasn't the time. He felt around for his clothes. "You expecting anyone?"

He cursed his carelessness and swore as he found his jeans and boxers. A year working a desk job and he was getting soft. Losing his edge.

Molly scrambled off the bed and flew to the dresser. "I don't normally get middle of the night visitors, if that's what you're implying." She yanked some clothes out of the drawer, tossing a sweatshirt on over the t-shirt and pulled on a pair of jeans.

Sam paused as he zipped his jeans. He'd said something wrong, but he had no time to figure out what it was.

He trailed her to the kitchen. Where was his gun? He'd been too sick the first day to think about it, but today, he should have checked it—kept it by his side. He recalled seeing Molly stick it on top of the fridge and felt for it. When his hand met the leather holster, he let out a breath of relief. What kind of cop was he to lose track of his weapon? He didn't like to wear the holster over bare skin, but it wouldn't be the first time. He shrugged into it, ignoring the burn as it settled over his wound.

He covered Molly's hand as she went to flick on the kitchen light. "No. See who it is first," he whispered.

Nodding, she pulled the curtain aside and her shoulders relaxed. "It's just Johnny."

He caught her arm before she could unlock the door. "Is he alone?"

Her eyes flashed and she shrugged. "I didn't see anyone else."

He stood beside the door, his back to the wall, gun in hand. "Ask him."

Before she could, Johnny pounded on the door again. "Molly, let me in! Quick!"

Molly shrugged off Sam's restraining hand. "He's my brother." She yanked the door open, and Johnny barreled in, turned and shut the door with a slam.

"Johnny! What in the world are you thinking? You're going to wake up Kelsie."

"Sorry, Molls, I need some money. I gotta get out of town." His words tumbled over one another and he peered out the window as he spoke.

"What? Why?" She turned the light on and Sam saw the pure panic on Johnny's face as he backed from the door.

"I don't have time to explain, I just need, I don't know, maybe a thousand dollars."

Molly's eyes widened. "I don't have a thousand dollars just lying around."

"Sit down." Sam stepped forward, grabbed Johnny by the scruff of his neck and pushed him onto a kitchen chair. "Now, spill it."

Johnny shrugged off Sam's hand with an annoyed glare, but he didn't hesitate to lay out the problem. "Those guys who shot at me the other night showed up at my apartment and said they'd kill me unless I came up with either a million dollars or the drugs. They said the other night was just a warning."

"What are you talking about? Why did they come to you?"

Johnny's eyes shifted as he squirmed in the chair. "Last winter, I was in a different biker club, and I was supposed to arrange transport of a shipment of coke, but I messed it up and the mule was caught at the border." His voice cracked as he continued, "How was I supposed to know that one of the balloons would pop?"

Molly sat, her face stunned. "You had someone swallow balloons filled with cocaine? A million dollars' worth?"

Johnny leaned towards his sister. "I didn't want to, Molls, I didn't, but someone was going to do it, so I figured I might as well get the credit, right?" He reached for her hand, but she shook him off.

"How could you, Johnny? I knew you were no angel, but I was a blind idiot to what you'd been doing. Get out of my house!" She stood and pointed at the door. "Now!"

"I didn't have much choice, Molly. When the Enforcer tells you to do something like that, you can't say no. I just wanted to ride with the club —I didn't want to deal drugs."

"Wait." Sam braced his arms on the table and leaned into Johnny's face. "Why did you look out the window when you came in? Were you expecting company?"

Johnny head bobbed as his eyes slid away from Sam's. "Yeah. They might have followed me. I'm not sure though."

"Oh my god. Kelsie." Molly's eyes shot to Sam's. He shouldn't have told her about his son. He could see her thinking it through, making the connections, wondering if they'd do to Kelsie what was done to Sean.

Anger shot through him. "And you led them right to your sister's house. A house where your six-year old niece lives." Sam shoved away from the table and raked a hand through his hair before he turned back to Johnny. "What were you *thinking?*" He was half-tempted to shoot the kid where he sat. The damn fool.

"I don't know. I guess I wasn't."

"No, you're just an idiot who's trying to feel important, and when you screw up, you run back to your big sis." Sam took a deep breath. He had to think—he could kick the kid's ass later. "Okay, here's what we have to do. We have to get Molly and Kelsie somewhere safe."

"Where?" Molly paced the kitchen, her arms crossed as though trying to keep warm. She trembled and he knew it was fear, but guessed it wasn't for herself.

"I know somewhere. Go pack enough clothes for at least a week. Just toss it all in a suitcase, we don't have much time."

Molly nodded and hurried down the hall.

"What about me?" Johnny jumped up and peeked out the windows. "Any minute, they could show up and kill me." Sweat beaded his brow

"Listen, you worm, they're not going to kill you until they have a chance of getting their demands met, so I give you a few days at least. After that?" Sam shrugged. Something about Johnny's story didn't ring true, but there wasn't time to unravel the mystery right now. "It's up to your sister if you go with us. I'm all for leaving your sorry ass here to face the music."

Sam went to the living room and removed the holster just long enough to put on a t-shirt. He donned socks then worked his feet into his boots. He regretted that he'd have to leave his bike here. Wait, maybe he could have Johnny follow them on Sam's bike. It was different from Johnny's, if Sam's hazy memory of that night was accurate. No biker would mistake the two. Not only that, it might buy them some time if they thought Johnny was still here because his bike was parked in plain view.

He wished he had a jacket to cover up his gun, but he could get one later. There was nothing of his to pack, just the clothes he wore and the small bag of new clothes. He grabbed that and put it on the kitchen table and made sure his wallet was in his jeans.

Molly's voice carried from Kelsie's room. Sam strode down the hall, stopping in the doorway. The little girl sat up in her bed, rubbing her eyes and blinking. Molly was trying her best to soothe her and still pack at the same time.

Sam took the pink duffle bag from Molly. "I'll finish this if you want to get her dressed."

Molly started to protest, but Sam interrupted. "I know what kid's need. Don't worry."

She nodded and took a stack of clothes off the dresser as she ushered Kelsie across the hall to the bathroom.

Sam stuffed the bag, making sure to get a mix so he didn't end up with all jeans and no shirts or the other way around. He looked in the closet, found some extra shoes and a jacket to add to the bag, then turned around. Kelsie would want some favorite toys, but he wasn't sure which ones those were. The stuffed dog on the bed was a sure bet, along with a well-worn blanket. The nightstand had some books that looked like they'd been read many times, so he took those too.

Molly came out of the bathroom with a cosmetic bag in one hand, and the other clutching the hand of a sleepy, cranky Kelsie. "Come on, hon, you can go back to sleep in the car."

"Where are we going?"

Sam zipped up the bag and met them in the hall. He winked at Kelsie. "We're going where the wild things are."

His attempt at humor backfired when Kelsie turned and pressed her face against Molly's side. "I don't wanna go, Mommy."

"Kels, it's okay. We're just going on a little trip. That's all."
With a hand on Kelsie's back, she herded her towards the
kitchen.

Sam snatched up the overnight bag that Molly had left
outside her door and followed behind them, plans hatching in
his mind.

Kelsie stopped suddenly and Sam almost crashed into
them. With a suspicious look cast towards him, she tugged on
Molly's arm. "Is Mr. Sam kitten-napping us?"

It felt like a bull rammed Sam's chest.

Molly darted a horrified glance over her shoulder at Sam,
and turned back, smoothing Kelsie's hair off her forehead. "Oh
no, hon. Nothing like that. An emergency came up and we have
to leave. Uncle Johnny is here too. He's out in the kitchen."

As Kelsie rushed into Johnny's arms, Molly turned and
whispered, "Sorry, Sam. I don't know where she learned about
kidnapping."

Sam shook his head. "No need to apologize. You have a
very smart little girl. She knows something isn't right and I'm a
stranger—she's drawing pretty good conclusions based on the
information she has."

Molly gave his arm a squeeze and offered an apologetic
smile. "Still…"

He bit his lip and nodded. Maybe it was her job training,
but he loved how she touched him to emphasize her words. Just
a pat here, or a squeeze there, but the contact was something he
hadn't had in a long time. He wished he could take her in his
arms, tell her how much tonight had meant to him.

Johnny held Kelsie on one arm and the little girl rested her
head on his shoulder. Sam felt envy creep over him. Johnny
didn't deserve her devotion, but Sam wasn't cruel enough to
crush Kelsie's obvious hero worship of her uncle. It gave him
another idea though.

The guys who were after Johnny could be waiting at the end of the drive. They needed a distraction.

Molly rummaged through some kitchen drawers, pulling out envelopes, papers and an address book. At Sam's questioning look, she explained, "My important papers, just in case something happens to the house."

Sam nodded. She hadn't said it, but he was sure she was thinking of his mother's house and how it had been set afire.

After tucking the papers into her purse, she asked, "Do you know how long we're going to be gone?"

"No, I'm sorry. It could be a few days, it could be longer." Sam's goal had been to find the enforcer to avenge the deaths of his son and mother, but he hadn't expected the gang to literally come to him. He could use this to his advantage, but he hated that Molly and Kelsie could be in danger. His first order of business was to get them safely to his cabin in the woods. Then come back and finish his business.

Taking the man off the streets would break the gang, at least for a while. The rest of the gang members would scatter like roaches under lights. Only then would Molly and Kelsie be safe.

She sighed. "Then I'm going to take everything I can."

Sam figured that was a wise decision and just nodded. He turned back to Johnny. "Give me your bike key."

The younger man shifted Kelsie to rest on this other arm as he fished in his pocket. He didn't hand it over immediately, instead, his eyes narrowed. "What for? I thought we were taking Molly's car."

"You and the ladies are, but your friends are going to be watching for a motorcycle to leave, so I'm going to give them that." At this point, they would only be keeping tabs on Johnny, not necessarily intend to kill him yet. They'd had the chance to kill him already and had let him go. No. A dead Johnny did them no good. Sam had a feeling that not all the cocaine had been inside the mule. Johnny might have kept a little aside for his own profit and the Ravens had figured it out and wanted to get it back.

Sam prayed they hadn't targeted Molly and Kelsie yet, but he knew if they weren't stopped, it was only a matter of time. He knew that firsthand.

"You're going to pretend to be me?"

Was that hope in Johnny's voice. Sam hid the disgust he felt. "Yeah. I want to try and draw them away before they ever see Molly and Kelsie." It was risky. If it didn't work, he'd have to double back and make sure they didn't follow Molly's car. "How many were there?"

"Two of them that I saw." Johnny hiked Kelsie higher and rubbed her back when the little girl woke up and protested the movement. "Shhhh, hon. It's okay." She relaxed and Johnny kissed the top of her head.

Sam grudgingly admitted that Johnny's affection for his niece seemed genuine. For her sake, and Molly's, Sam would do his best to keep Johnny in one piece, and keep him out of prison at the same time. It wasn't going to be an easy task. The kid might be safer in a cell than on the streets.

Sam spotted a pen on the counter. "Molly, do you have some paper? I'll write out directions to where we can meet up."

She opened her purse and took a small note pad out. "Here you go."

"Thanks." Sam jotted down the information. "I'll try and get there first, but if I'm not there, go ahead and go into the cabin. There's a key under the third flowerpot in the window box."

Sam took out his wallet. He didn't want to do this in front of Johnny but there was no way around it. He counted out five hundred dollars, keeping a few hundred for himself. Long ago, he'd learned to carry cash for emergencies. It was untraceable and with enough of it, people could vanish without a paper trail. "Molly, take this, in case we get separated. Follow the directions carefully as the road has a lot of twists and turns. When you reach the lake, take a left. The road parallels the lake, but at one point, it angles back towards the woods. When it does, look for a brown A-frame. It's hard to see at night, but there's a red mailbox on a post by the road." Sam drew a sketch of the house and an approximation of the twists and turns to get to it.

"The cabin might not look like much, but it's solid, and it's hard to find if you don't know the area." Sam was about to hand her the note, but then pulled it back. "Damn. I forgot all the utilities will be shut off. It's just a matter of flipping some switches in the fuse box and turning the water valve. Normally it's easy to do because I usually arrive in the middle of the day. At night, it's trickier because the box is on the wall in the laundry room, which will be pitch black when you arrive."

"I have a flashlight in the car."

"Perfect." He handed her the directions. "Just flip the main circuit breaker—it's labeled."

Molly nodded, but raised her gaze from the paper to latch onto Sam's face, her brow furrowed in concern. "You make it sound like you won't be there?"

Sam didn't want to frighten her, but if the Ravens thought they were making a break for it, he'd have to make sure the bikers didn't follow them and he damn well wasn't going to let them follow a mother and child, no matter what happened to him. "Listen, Molly. Those guys out there, they aren't playing games. However, I know their tactics. I was one of them for a year."

"What? When?" Johnny stepped up to the counter.

Sam barely spared him a glance as he tapped the paper with the address. "The cabin belonged to my grandfather on my mother's side. When my mother…was killed…I inherited it, but I haven't yet had to pay real estate taxes, so it won't show up anywhere under my name. I keep it stocked with non-perishables as a safeguard. Everything you need for up to a month is right there."

Molly's eyes widened in alarm. "Sam, I have a job. Kelsie has school. We have a life right here. What am I supposed to do? Just leave it all?"

"I know how hard this is. Believe me, and I'm only looking at the worst case scenario. In all likelihood, this won't take more than a few days."

Molly looked from Johnny to Sam, her eyes flashing. "This is crazy."

Sam hated that they'd been dragged into this mess. The last thing he ever wanted to do was put more innocents in harm's way and even though Johnny was at fault this time, he couldn't help thinking that if he had brought down the Ravens a year ago, none of this would be happening. He stepped close and drew her against him. "I know it's crazy. I'm sorry."

Molly returned the hug, but only for a moment before she stepped out of his embrace. "Okay. Fine. Let's get this over with—the sooner the better. I guess Kelsie can miss the last few days of school."

Johnny pushed in front of Sam, his mouth twisted into a sneer. "You and Molly got a thing going on? Is that why there's the rush to get her to your conveniently stocked house in the woods?"

The guy had balls, Sam had to give him credit for that. Too bad God hadn't given him more than two brain cells to go along with them. He moved alongside Johnny, the side opposite from Kelsie, and kept his voice low as he said in Johnny's ear, "Listen, you little turd, it's none of your damn business what goes on between me and your sister. Now, get the hell out there and drive them to safety."

Johnny's bravado wilted at Sam's tone. "Whatever. I'm taking Kelsie out to the car."

Molly and Sam exchanged cellphone numbers and despite the dire circumstances, he felt a rush of pleasure knowing he could contact her. "Sorry about that scene with your brother."

Molly sighed. "I can't figure out what he's so touchy about. He should be happy—after all, he's constantly trying to set me up with his biker friends."

Sam didn't like the sound of that, but didn't have time to pursue the topic.

Five minutes later, he tucked the blanket around Kelsie as Molly and Johnny got in the front seat of Molly's SUV. He gently shut the door and moved to Molly's window. "Give me a few minutes to walk the bike up towards the road. I want to take a look around and with a little luck, nobody is waiting. If everything looks clear, I'll call you and let it ring once then hang up. No need to answer. I'll take a right out of here and do the same at the next intersection. If I feel the way isn't clear, I'll let it ring twice. That will mean stay put until I do the one ring call again. I'll try and draw them away. If I can't, I'll come back and we'll think up something else."

Molly nodded and gave him a half-wave as she rolled up the window. Sam limped to Johnny's bike. It was a sportster and he didn't think he'd have any problem wheeling it to the end of the drive. Its speed might come in handy too. His own bike was heavier, but would be more comfortable on a long ride. No matter, this would do. The rustle of gravel under the tires made him cringe and wish the driveway was paved. As he came to the end, he paused every few feet to listen. All he heard was the chirping of crickets, the far off sound of a dog barking and the zing and crackle of bugs flying into the bug zapper in the front yard. All clear. He let out a deep breath and tried not to get his hopes up. Sitting right at the end of the driveway probably wasn't something even boneheaded Johnny would do. He straddled the motorcycle, and pulled out the cell, hitting the quick dial for Molly's phone. He clicked end after one ring and started the motorcycle and hung a right onto the road.

The country highway was empty and dark at this time of night, only the moon's glow competing with his headlight. He rode slowly, partially to make sure nobody was following and also to get used to Johnny's bike. Stretching for the handlebars tugged at the wound on his back, but it was bearable. Rolling his shoulders, he grunted as the muscles loosened and the pain decreased. At the first intersection, he stopped and examined the crossroad for any sign of a trap. Nothing. He sent the signal to Molly's phone.

It would take them a few minutes to catch up to him, so he drove a few hundred feet down each side of the crossroad. The cornfields hugged the road, and Sam hated how they seemed to close in over him. The fields would be the perfect hiding spot for a few bikes, but as far as he could tell, it was clear in both directions.

When he returned to the intersection, Johnny was just pulling up. Sam waved and took the lead. They drove for ten minutes without incident. The highway was just ahead and Sam turned onto the frontage road to get to an entrance ramp. He slowed as they approached. The ramp appeared empty but something about the shape of a bush just off the shoulder seemed off. At the last second, he swerved back onto the frontage road. He couldn't have pinpointed exactly what it was if someone had asked him, but he'd learned to trust his instincts, so he swerved and hoped Johnny would follow.

The kid must have been paying attention for once because he stayed to the frontage road. In Sam's mirror, he saw two lights head the wrong way down the ramp and turn onto the road going in the same direction as Sam was heading.

"Shit!" Sam crossed the center-line and waved for Johnny to pass him. No way was he going to let those guys come up behind Molly and Kelsie. He swerved back into his lane, glad that Johnny had sped up, but worried about Johnny getting in an accident. It wouldn't do much good to stop the bad guys if they got killed in the process.

Sam slowed, allowing Johnny to create a large gap between them. The guys tailing them would have to make a decision to either follow him, or the car. For all Sam knew, they weren't even interested in the car. If they didn't know what kind Molly had, they might disregard it.

Just as he'd hoped, Johnny took the next exit. Sam stayed on the frontage road and watched the riders behind him hesitate at the entrance ramp but then pass it by. They gunned their bikes and he did the same. Sam couldn't help the thrill that shot through him. The speed and the danger was intoxicating. It was his vice. His weakness. If he was a normal guy, he'd be content with a desk job.

The motorcycles giving chase were choppers, and while cool, they were no match for the crotch rocket Sam rode. He didn't want to get too far ahead though. Not until Johnny had a chance to put some highway between them.

Ten minutes later, Sam allowed the choppers to get close, then he headed towards a boarded up gas station and pulled in. Running was fine when there was no choice, but now that Molly and Kelsie were safely away, he had to take a stand.

He made a U-turn around the capped gas pumps and faced the two choppers as they pulled into the station. Gun ready in his hand, but pointing down, he waited to see what they would do. He had no doubt he could pluck them off their bikes with a shot to the chest if need be. If they got him in return, then so be it. These guys may not be the ones who ordered the hit on his mother and son, but they worked for him.

The bikers seemed confused at Sam's sudden switch from running to standing, and they stopped about ten feet from him. He hoped he'd recognize them from his time in the gang, but they were strangers to him. One wore a dew rag and sported an impressive gut. The other had a scraggly ponytail and even in the dim light from a half-moon, showed evidence of an ongoing battle with bad skin. Buddha and Pimple.

Buddha pulled closer, squinting at Sam before shaking his head. "Look, dude, we thought you were somebody else."

"Flea?"

Buddha's eyes opened wide. "Yeah."

Sam nodded. "Well, your surveillance or whatever the hell you've been ordered to do, ends now."

Pimple laughed. "We don't take no orders from you, asshole."

Sam forced a laugh. "Yeah? Well, I don't blame you. That scumbag you take orders from wouldn't hesitate to murder your firstborn if you disobey."

Pimple appeared to think about that, as though puzzled. "I ain't got no kids."

Sam rolled his eyes. "Okay, so that leaves your mother, siblings, hell, even your dog, but I don't give a shit about that." And idea hit him and he went with it. "I'm giving you a message to take back to Howard."

Buddha's uni-brow raised in surprise at Sam's use of the enforcer's real name. It wasn't something commonly known, but this guy obviously was part of the inner circle. Good. That meant Howard would get the message for sure.

The surprise changed to belligerence and Buddha opened his mouth, but Sam cut off whatever he was going to say. "You tell him that Flea's debt is paid in full. If he doesn't accept that, tell him that Sam Brennan came to collect a debt, but I'll take the forgiveness of Flea's debt and call it even." It killed him to let

Sean's killer off so easily, but if it saved Molly and Kelsie, it'd be worth it. "If he declines the offer, tell him I'll find him and collect what he owes me. The only currency I'll recognize will be his blood."

Before either could respond, Sam aimed his gun at Buddha's back tire and pulled the trigger. Both Ravens ducked as Sam fired another shot at the ground. As much as he wanted to kill them, they had an important message to deliver. Satisfied by the mass of rubber that had been Buddha's tire, Sam gunned the throttle and roared away.

* * *

Molly nudged Johnny, while keeping one hand tight on the wheel. "Hey, wake up!"

Johnny groaned and turned away. "I'm tired."

He was tired? Molly rolled her eyes. She'd been driving the last three hours while her brother had snoozed. She shoved her brother's shoulder. "You need to watch for the cabin." Luckily, Kelsie had slept most of the drive, but she'd be waking up in the next few hours, and Molly wanted to find the cabin and get at least a little sleep before Kelsie woke up for the day.

Johnny stretched. "Fine." He sat up and took the paper Molly thrust in his face. "What's this? The address?"

"Yeah. Look for that road Sam said we needed to turn onto."

He leaned forward and squinted up at a passing sign. Moonlight danced through a canopy of treetops, the light and shade making it difficult to read the signs. "Naw, that's not it."

It wouldn't be long before the sun rose but she'd hoped to find the house before that. Once sunlight hit Kelsie's eyes, she was awake for the day. She felt Johnny watching her and glanced at him. "What?"

Johnny got a sly look on his face. "So, what's going on with you and Sam?"

"Nothing." Her answer had been too quick and she knew it. The heat of a blush warmed her cheeks.

"Yeah. Right."

Molly decided that she didn't owe her brother an explanation, but she didn't want to appear ashamed either. She was a grown woman. She certainly didn't need her brother's approval. "Sam and I talked last night. I learned some things about him and see him in a different light. That's all."

"Is he a cop?"

"Why would you ask that?"

Johnny shrugged. "The way he was back at your house. He's bossy, just like a cop."

"Bossy? By that, do you mean he took charge? Then yeah, I'd agree he did that. Somebody had to." She was tired, scared and way too cranky to attempt any semblance of politeness. "Johnny, do you ever think of anyone but yourself?"

He sulked with his head against the window and then pointed ahead. "I think that's the road."

Molly turned her attention to driving and made the turn. The trees hugged the gravel road, and she wondered if they should have just stayed at a motel for the night and met Sam here later. Well, it was too late for that now. "Is this it?"

Johnny looked at the paper in his hand. "Yeah. Looks like it."

After parking alongside the cabin, Molly took Kelsie from her seat, and steered the sleepy child up porch steps. Johnny took the flashlight out of the glove box and retrieved the key exactly where Sam said it would be. She wished he was here. It felt strange to go into someone else's house even though he'd sent them there.

Five minutes later, they had electricity as Johnny found the circuit breakers. The house had a closed-up odor of mustiness, but otherwise appeared clean and well-kept. Molly led Kelsie to the bathroom, and afterwards, checked out each of the three bedrooms, feeling a little bit like Goldilocks as on the third try, she found a room with a twin bed instead of the queen beds she'd found in the previous two rooms. The bed was made up with a blue comforter decorated with red rocket ships. Sean's bed? She hoped it was okay to use, but Sam hadn't put anything off limits.

She tucked Kelsie in, praying her little girl would sleep a few more hours. It was the only way she'd get any sleep. She and Johnny had traded driving for a little while, so she'd caught a catnap, but she was exhausted. It was one of the longest nights of her life.

Johnny helped himself to one room and shut the door. That left her with the one remaining room. She cast a glance at the sofa, and decided to sleep there for now. When Sam came in, he'd be tired too. She glanced out the window, hoping to see him ride up, but the woods were pitch black as if someone had dropped a black velvet curtain around the house.

Was he okay? Had he been able to shake the Ravens following him? Her cell. She had his number. She grabbed her purse and found her phone and the paper with his number. It went to voice-mail on the fourth ring.

The clock on the stove said it was almost four a.m. In another hour, the sun would be up. Thoughts of sleep vanished in her worry for Sam. What if the Ravens caught him? Would they hurt him? She sat on the edge of the sofa, her hands folded over the phone and her elbows on her knees. Her back ached and she sighed as her muscles, stiff from driving so long, finally demanded relief. She leaned back against the couch, but didn't intend to fall asleep.

* * *

Sam parked the bike and trudged up the steps to the door. It was locked. *Shit.* He rattled the doorknob and peeked in the window beside the door. Molly's hair was visible on the end of the couch, but she didn't budge when he tapped softly. It hadn't occurred to him that everyone would be asleep and the house locked up. He couldn't remember ever being in the house when the door was locked.

There was nothing else to do but knock again, harder this time. Just as he feared, Molly shot off the couch like a cat with its tail on fire, and he chuckled at the sight of her hair sticking out in every direction. It took her a moment to get her bearings before she stumbled to the door, blinking out at him through the window before opening the door.

Sam stepped into the house. "You made it. Have any trouble?" He tucked a wayward curl behind her ear, happy for an excuse to touch her.

She shook her head but her eyes met his and welled with tears.

Still touching her hair, he slid his hand behind her neck and pulled her against his chest. She trembled, her face pressed against his throat. He kneaded the tense muscles at the base of her neck. "Shhhh…it's okay."

It had been a helluva night and he understood her need for a few minutes to compose herself. He was bone-tired, his back ached and his leg throbbed, but he hadn't had to pick up and leave his home without a clue where he was going. By meeting him here, she'd offered up her trust to him. Trust that he'd keep her daughter safe.

Molly pulled back and put her fingers to the corners of her eyes, swiping the lingering tears away. "I was worried and I tried to call, but you didn't answer your cell. The last time I saw you, guys on motorcycles were chasing you down the highway."

Sam took a deep breath and let it out slowly. "It's fine. I gave them a warning—that's all, but just in case they had others looking for me, I took a couple of detours. That's why I'm late." He limped to the sofa and sat heavily, biting back a groan.

She nodded and crossed her arms. "Sorry about…that."

He paused in the act of rolling his shoulders to work out a kink. "What?"

"The…tears. I'm just tired, I guess."

"You've had a crazy night. There's no shame in spilling a few tears." He swung his legs up and pivoted to lie down, crossing his feet, boots and all, on the opposite arm of the sofa. "Why don't you go try to get some sleep for a few hours." It felt so good to stretch out and his eyes started closing of their own volition.

He started at a squeak from the rocking chair a few feet away. He tilted his head to see Molly leaning back in it. "Aren't you gonna get some shut-eye?"

She shook her head. "I'm tired, but too keyed up to sleep." Both hands gripped the arms of the chair as it rocked gently. "This has to be the craziest twenty-four hours in my life." Her lips pressed together as she took a deep breath, slanting him a look. "What happened last evening…that should probably never happen again."

Sam pushed up to a sitting position, not caring if the thump of his feet hitting the hardwood floor awoke the others. He hadn't forgotten what they'd shared. The memory had carried him through the hours riding the black ribbon of highway to the cabin. "Are you sorry you slept with me? Because I'm not sorry. Not one little bit. No matter what happens from here on out, what we shared meant a lot to me." He ran a hand through his matted hair, flattened from his helmet. Being with Molly had been the best thing that had happened to him since before his son died.

She held his gaze for a moment before breaking eye contact. "I'm not sorry, Sam. It's just...I have Kelsie to think about. I can't get involved with a man who is going to ride out of my life as suddenly as he rode into it." One shoulder rose in a half-shrug. "I'm not blaming you. I wasn't thinking last night but now I've had time to realize that it would never work between us."

Sam opened his mouth with an assurance that he wouldn't ride out on her poised on the tip of his tongue, but he snapped his mouth shut. It wasn't a promise he could keep. With so much up in the air, he didn't even know what tomorrow would bring let alone a month or two down the road. His weariness seemed to triple as if a lead blanket had fallen over his shoulders. He scrubbed his hand down his face and nodded. "I wouldn't intend to do that, but you're right, it could happen."

Molly stood. "I can sleep with Kelsie while we're here."

Sam nodded reluctantly. "Did you put her in the big room with the queen-sized bed?"

"No, she's in the one with the rocket ships." Her voice took on a worried tone.

He saw the unasked question written on her face. "Yes, it was Sean's room, and it's fine that Kelsie is sleeping there."

His son had been a generous kid and would have volunteered his bed if he'd been here. Sean would have thought it an adventure to sleep on the couch instead. The familiar pain settled in Sam's chest. For a little while, the ache had faded, but now it rose fierce and strong, twisting his heart as if punishing him for forgetting about it. He cleared his throat before speaking again, "It's okay to sleep there, but you would be more comfortable in the big bed in my room." He hurried to add, "I'd sleep in Sean's room. You and Kelsie can have the big bed."

Molly nodded. "If we're still here tomorrow night—" She broke off, her brow creased in confusion. "Or I guess that's tonight...anyway, next time we go to sleep, if we're still here, we'll take the big bed. I don't want to wake her now."

"Fine." Sam rose, wincing at the various aches and pains as he shuffled to his room.

CHAPTER FIVE

"Mommy, I'm hungry."

Molly groaned into the pillow. It seemed like she'd just shut her eyes. "Okay, honey. Just give Mommy a sec, okay?"

Kelsie shook her shoulder. "Can I go play on the beach?"

That got Molly's attention. "No, not yet. You have to wait until I can go out there with you."

There was no way she'd get another moment of shut-eye. Not with a curious little girl in the house and a lake just a stone's throw away. She swung her feet off the bed and sat on the edge for a moment, rubbing her eyes. Rising, she padded out to the kitchen to see what she could rummage up for breakfast. Sam was correct when he'd said the pantry was stocked, but most of the food was canned vegetables, soups, tuna, rice, and pasta. There wasn't a Cheerio in sight. *Shoot.* Molly brushed her hair out of her eyes with one hand as she stared into the pantry as if by looking long enough, a box of cereal would magically appear. Sighing when that didn't work, she went back to the bedroom and rummaged through her suitcase for clean clothes. Kelsie bounced behind her, chattering as only she knew how, asking how long they were staying, if she could swim in the lake or roast marshmallows after dinner.

"Kels, I need to wake up first, and you know to do that, I need to shower." She unzipped Kelsie's bag and grabbed some clothes for her too. "Come on, hon. Why don't you get dressed and brush your teeth while I shower? Then we can go to the store—wherever it is—and buy some stuff for a big breakfast."

Always up for a trip to the store, Kelsie agreed and thirty minutes later, they were both ready to go. Only Molly had no idea where the nearest store might be. She needed some directions first. She stood outside Sam's room, hesitant to wake him, but there was nothing else she could do.

Molly knocked, and waited. Nothing. She rapped again, harder this time. Nothing. She tried the doorknob and opened the door far enough to stick her head in. Sam lay sprawled on the bed, bare from the waist up, the covers draped over his hips. Heat rushed up her cheeks. "Sam?"

He finally stirred and rose up on his elbows, the sheet dipping into dangerous territory. "Yeah?"

There wasn't a shred of embarrassment on his face while Molly was sure hers radiated enough heat to boil a teapot.

"I was just wondering where the closest store is? Kelsie's hungry, so I need to get something."

"Oh. Yeah." He turned and swung his legs over the side of the bed, standing.

Molly began to look away until she realized he was wearing sweatpants. Relief mixed with disappointment. She shook that last feeling off.

"I'll get dressed and join you."

"Oh, no. That's okay. You must be exhausted. I just need you to point me in the right direction."

"Don't worry, I'm a pro at lack of sleep." He scratched his flat, washboard stomach, drawing her eye there.

He didn't appear to notice the direction of her gaze as he gave her a lopsided grin that shot straight to her heart. "There are some things I need to get anyway. I'll only be a few minutes."

Sam brushed past as he exited the room. His scent washed over her and now that she had exquisite memories to associate with it, she had to remind herself that she had slammed the door on any repeat performances.

Flustered and confused, she tried to shake it off as she directed Kelsie to get her shoes on. Molly found a hairband in her purse and pulled her still damp curls into a ponytail. Finally feeling awake, she started making a mental list of what she should get, and wondered if Johnny had any requests.

She knocked on Johnny's door then stuck her head in, not waiting for an invitation to open the door. "Hey, Johnny. We're all going to the store to get some groceries."

He waved an acknowledgment and rolled over.

"Well, I guess you don't need anything." Miffed at his lack of response, she shut the door harder than she intended.

"Is something wrong?"

Sam stood in the hallway, a towel around his waist. Molly averted her eyes. This was going to be a lot more difficult than she expected. "No, sorry about that. Just frustrated." She shrugged and tried to grin. *"Brothers"*

Sam's gaze moved from the top of her head and down her body. She suppressed a shiver at the intimate appraisal. As she watched him, a drop of water trickled from his hair in a winding trail down his throat, across his chest, to disappear into the terry cloth. *Lucky drop.* This was going to be agony. "Are you going to be long? Kelsie's starving."

She probably sounded like a shrew and embarrassed, she didn't wait for a reply, just exited the cabin to find out where Kelsie had disappeared. The land sloped unevenly to a sandy beach. The woods around the house looked thick with tangled undergrowth, and she didn't think her daughter would go there, not with a lake in view. Shielding her eyes, she spotted Kelsie skipping along the shore, a long stick in one hand. Every few skips, she'd stop to poke at something in the sand.

"Kelsie!"

The skipping ceased and Kelsie raced towards her, when she got close, she shouted, "Mommy! I found a shell!" She opened a palm to show Molly an ugly brown snail.

"Oh, that's beautiful, hon, but we have to go to town to get some groceries and breakfast."

"Okay. Can we come back here? Can I go swimming later? Can I build a sandcastle?"

Molly laughed at the rapid fire questions and tousled Kelsie's hair. "Sure, later this afternoon."

By the time they got back to the cabin, Sam was stepping onto the front deck. His hair was still damp, and he wore a black polo shirt. It wasn't one she'd bought, so it must have been one he had here. It looked good on him.

"Ready to go?" Sam limped down the steps.

"Yeah, I just have to grab my purse." Molly gave Kelsie a gentle push towards the car. "Hop in and buckle up. I'll be right out."

Kelsie nodded, but turned back. "Are you coming too, Mr. Sam?"

"Sure am, sweetheart."

Molly loved how Sam spoke to Kelsie, but worried about her daughter growing close to him. One of Kelsie's favorite games to play with her stuffed animals was to have wedding ceremonies and create perfect little families. Molly grabbed her purse from the floor where she'd dropped it and hurried back to the car.

Sam directed her to the main road, and she was grateful he'd come along. The road turned and wound through the forest, with other roads connecting and she was lost after the third turn. "Holy cow, Sam. How do you find your way around here?"

He laughed. "I've been coming up here all my life."

"It's really beautiful." Molly had lived in Wisconsin her whole life, but rarely ventured north of Madison. "You know, I don't think I've ever been this far north in the state before." She slanted a grin at Sam. "Pretty sad, huh?"

"Seriously? That is sad."

"Well, my mom and stepdad loved taking me places like Washington D.C., Williamsburg or a couple of times, Disney World." She shrugged and tried to sound nonchalant when she continued, "When I went to live with my dad, well he wasn't big into vacations."

She felt Sam watching her and glanced at him. "What?"

His eyebrows went up and he spread his hands. "Nothing. I'm just sorry you missed out." He faced the front again and motioned at the canopy of trees. "I didn't realize how much I'd missed it. It's so...peaceful up here."

Molly had to agree. She glanced in the review mirror to see Kelsie with her nose pressed to the window. A pang of guilt poked her. How many times had she intended to take Kelsie away on vacation somewhere, but never did? Something always came up. Other than a couple of overnight trips to Chicago, Kelsie had been nowhere. No wonder she was so enthralled with her surroundings.

It was a twenty-five minute drive to town, but with no traffic, it didn't seem to take that long. The town consisted of one main street anchored at one end by a church, and a small medical center, and at the other by a grocery store across from a handful of restaurants. "So, what's the best place?"

Sam pointed at the second restaurant on the right. "I don't know about best, but they're fast, and I'm so hungry I could eat a bear."

"They have bears in there?" Kelsie sounded like she didn't know whether to be scared or excited at the prospect.

Sam laughed. "No. That's just an expression."

Molly parked in front of the restaurant and took Kelsie's hand as she exited. Sam held the door for them to enter first, and Molly told herself not to get used to the treatment. In her real life, a guy was just as likely to scamper through a door she'd just opened rather than offer the simple courtesy. The diner wasn't fancy. It had plain white tables adorned with paper placemats, chrome salt and pepper holders and laminated menus crammed between the ketchup and mustard bottles. The scents of eggs, bacon, coffee and pancakes mingled and vied for dominance and made up for any lack of ambience the décor offered. Sam led them to the back of the diner and put a hand on a chair for Molly, sliding it out for her, and then he patted a chair for Kelsie. "Have a seat, m'lady."

Kelsie giggled and plopped onto the seat in a very un-ladylike manner. Molly couldn't help but grin, and when Sam sat opposite her, the corners of his eyes still held the hint of his smile. He handed her a menu and opened his.

The waitress swept towards them, a full pot of coffee in one hand, a bottle of Tabasco sauce in the other. She deposited the sauce at the table across the aisle before rounding on them.

"How are you folks this morning, eh?" She waited for Sam to turn his cup over before filling it, then turned a questioning eye to Molly. "Coffee?"

"Please." It would take more than strong coffee to erase her fatigue, but it was a start. The waitress had a slim figure and her quick movement had fooled Molly into thinking the woman was younger, but a closer look showed the waitress was probably in her late-fifties. Molly hoped she looked as good when she was that age. Right now, she felt about a hundred. She barely stifled a yawn as the waitress filled her cup with fragrant brew.

"I'm Doreen, and I'll be back in a jiff to get your order."

Molly caught the surprised look on Sam's face when Doreen had said her name. "Is something wrong?"

Sam shook his head. "No..." He lifted one shoulder in half-shrug. "The waitress was one of my mom's friends. I guess she didn't recognize me."

Molly pulled a pencil out of her purse and handed it to Kelsie, who had begun fidgeting. "Here hon, why don't you draw me a picture?" She turned her attention to Sam. "When was the last time you saw her?"

"At the funerals." His tone belied the calm expression he wore as he studied his menu.

Her throat constricted for him. She cleared it and said, "Well, it's pretty busy in here. She probably didn't take a close look."

"Oh, I understand. I looked a lot different then. It's just that seeing her reminded me of all the summers I spent here."

"This town is so peaceful. I bet you have a ton of great memories." After her parents had been killed, she found it helped to remember the good times. Not at first—it was too painful—but eventually. It took a while, but she found that the pain that came with the good memories gradually faded, leaving just the happy feelings.

Sam grunted and took a sip of his coffee. Molly sighed and focused on the menu. She knew Kelsie would want pancakes and bacon with a glass of milk. For herself, she thought scrambled eggs sounded good, with hash browns. She could always steal a bite of Kelsie's pancake to quiet her sweet tooth.

"You folks ready to order?"

Molly went first, then Sam. When he finished, Doreen lowered her pad of paper and looked over her half-glasses. "Sammy? Is that you?"

He nodded. "Yeah. How are you doing, Doreen?"

"Come here and give me a hug." She tucked her pad in the back pocket of her jeans. "How are you holding up? You look like you've lost weight."

Sam's face colored, but he stood and wrapped his arms around her. His eyes closed for a moment and when he opened them, Molly saw they were bright. He blinked and said, "I'm okay." He patted his flat belly. "I'd gained weight for the undercover job, but always planned to drop it." His voice became grim. "It was easier than I thought it would be."

Doreen snorted. "Yeah, well, grief will do that to you. When my William passed on, I lost twenty pounds."

Sam just nodded, but then must have remembered his manners. "Doreen, this is Molly and her daughter, Kelsie."

Doreen eyed Molly with reserve, but held out her hand. "Nice to meet you, Molly."

Molly returned the handshake. "Doreen." Why was she sensing hostility from the older woman?

Doreen leaned over Kelsie and exclaimed about the beautiful picture. Kelsie beamed and Molly chalked up the hostility to her imagination.

When the food came, they were all too hungry to talk. Even Kelsie ate without her usual chatter. When the bill came, Molly reached for her purse hanging on the back of her chair, but Sam waved her off.

When she started to protest, he said, "I'll get it, Molly. I dragged you all the way up here and you wouldn't have this expense if it weren't for me."

It was on the tip of her tongue to remind him that her brother had instigated everything. Sure, he'd brought Sam to her door, but the Ravens would have been chasing him whether Sam had been at her house or not. She let the subject drop when Doreen approached and rested a hand on Sam's shoulder.

"Sammy, are you staying long? I'm sure some of the old gang would love to see you. Victoria got back in town last week." The woman leaned in as though telling a secret, but her voice was as loud as before when she said, "She and her husband split up, ya know."

Sam shrugged. "We haven't decided how long we'll be here, but tell Victoria I said hello and I'm sorry about her marriage. That's rough." He held an arm out for Molly and Kelsie to precede him to the front of the diner.

"I will. She'll be excited to see you again. She's been so upset that she couldn't make it to the funeral services." Doreen followed them to the door.

Molly turned at the words and saw Sam's eyes flicker with pain. Didn't Doreen realize how callous she sounded?

She must have opened her mouth to say something because Sam gave a swift shake of his head. The last thing she wanted to do was add to his discomfort, so she snapped her mouth closed and herded Kelsie back towards the car.

"We can leave the car parked here. The store is just across the street."

The store was tiny, not much bigger than a convenience store, but it still had all the usual departments, just on a smaller scale. Molly chose four apples, a bunch of bananas and a mango. Sam made a face when she asked if he wanted a mango too.

"Sorry—too slimy for me."

She laughed and shook her head. "Oh, but they're so sweet and juicy."

His eyebrow rose and a speculative gleam came to his eyes. "Mmm...sounds...delicious."

Something about his tone made her face burn and she glanced away. "Kelsie, put the pineapple back. Sponge Bob doesn't really live in one." Molly wouldn't have minded buying the pineapple but Kelsie never actually ate the fruit because she didn't like the texture.

Sam chuckled. "Hey Kelsie, do you want to split a pint of strawberries with me?"

Kelsie put the pineapple back and scampered around the shopping cart to stand beside Sam. "I love strawberries!"

"Smart girl." He put a pint in the cart and looked directly at Molly. "I wonder if these are sweet and juicy?"

Certain her cheeks were flaming, Molly cleared her throat and hurried out of the produce section.

They bought chicken and hamburger in the meat department, some staples, and Sam ran off and came back with two cartons of ice cream. One vanilla, the other Rocky Road. He held them up as if asking permission. She couldn't help laughing at his little boy expression. He tossed in graham crackers, marshmallows and chocolate bars. Molly covered them with a loaf of bread, not wanting Kelsie to see them just yet.

Molly never would have considered grocery shopping a form of intimacy, but seeing what kind of cereal, bread and vegetables Sam chose told her things about the man. He had a sweet tooth, but also had a penchant for carrots and broccoli.

They each carried a couple of bags and Kelsie had one bag light enough for her as they made their way back to the car.

Just as they added the last bag to the trunk, a woman sauntered across the street towards them. "Sammy!"

Sam turned and she caught a flash of annoyance in his expression before a polite smile replaced it. "How are you doing, Victoria?"

The woman stepped right up to Sam and flung her arms around him. "Oh Sammy, I was so sorry to hear about the loss of your mother and your son. I cried for days when I heard."

Sam returned the hug but his posture remained stiff. "Thank-you." He pulled her arms from around his neck and held her hands in front of him, like a politician on campaign tour. "I see you've spoken to your mother."

It didn't take a Rhodes Scholar to figure out that this woman was the recently divorced Victoria. She recognized a woman on the hunt when she saw one. Well, let her have him. It wasn't like Molly was looking for a man.

Molly shepherded Kelsie into the car, reminding her to buckle up. Then she took a few steps to the back of the car and touched Sam's arm to get his attention. She felt the strange urge to lean into him as she held her hand out to Victoria. "Hello. I'm Molly."

Victoria glanced at Molly as though seeing her for the first time then slowly took Molly's hand a brief shake. "I'm Victoria."

"Pleased to meet you." Flashing her teeth in what she hoped was a smile, Molly added, "We met your mother in the diner a little while ago. Lovely woman."

Sam's mouth quirked as if he were biting back a grin. It was all Molly could do to hold her own laughter in check.

Victoria's eyes narrowed as she glanced between the two, but her teeth gleamed as she ran her hands under her hair, lifting it into a loose ponytail. "It sure is hot out here today. I think a swim would feel delicious, don't you?"

Sam turned towards Molly and snapped his fingers. "Speaking of swimming, we need to stop by the gift shop and get a suit for Kelsie. Did you pack one for yourself?"

Molly hadn't planned on swimming, but something in the other woman's eyes goaded her to answer, "No, I didn't, but Victoria is right. The water would feel wonderful this afternoon." She smiled at Victoria. "But we'd better hurry before the ice cream melts."

"Right." Sam held out his hand to Victoria. "Well, it's been great seeing you again."

Victoria ignored his hand and threw her arms around his neck. "Oh, I'm sure we'll see each other again soon."

* * *

The air shimmered with heat, but Sam hardly noticed as he tried not to gawk at Molly in her red swimsuit. It was hardly revealing, with a modest scoop neck and a racer back, but it hugged her curves better than a Ferrari on a racetrack. He was glad for the dark sunglasses as he reclined on the Adirondack lounger and tracked her movements while appearing to be dozing. Molly had implored him to go in the water, but he'd resisted. The last time he'd gone swimming, it had been with his son. It didn't feel right to enjoy a swim. Not without Sean.

Molly hadn't pushed, but the sadness in her eyes forced him to pretend to find something fascinating on the far side of the lake. After a bit, Molly quit sending him concerned looks as she and Kelsie played in the water. He sighed and rested his head back. His muscles ached from last night's long drive and his eyes burned from lack of sleep. Closing them, he took a deep breath as the heat of the afternoon soaked into him.

As he relaxed, his pain eased and he recalled the sand castle he and Sean had built a year ago. It had been a doozy, complete with parapets and a moat. Sean had collected bits of wood along the water's edge to use as knights, planting them at intervals along the top of the castle. Sam had tossed pebbles at the castle in a barrage from the bad guys.

Sam smiled at the memory. Sean could have played that game for hours, but a late afternoon thunderstorm had cut it short and destroyed the castle. Sean hadn't minded though, and had already started planning the next one.

An infectious giggle drew him from his memories, and he smiled as Molly and Kelsie kicked water at each other before

Molly ran at Kelsie and swept her up, spinning her in a tight circle. Kelsie's little legs flew out as she shrieked in delight while Molly nuzzled her neck. "I caught you, you little imp." Molly faced Sam and held Kelsie at arm's length. "Look, Sam! I got the biggest fish in the lake!"

Sam grinned and played along. "Naw, I don't think so. I think you need to throw that little shrimp back." He planted his feet on either side of the chair, pushed to a standing position and headed for the water line. He winked at Molly as he raised his arms as if he wanted to take the little girl. "Yep, gotta toss that one far out into the lake. Don't want it coming back and stealing my bait again."

Kelsie tried to wriggle out of Molly's grasp as she eyed him in mock terror, but her shouts for help dissolved into laughter. The sound washed over him, as soothing as the cool water that lapped at his ankles.

Molly set Kelsie down and the little girl took off with her mother in pursuit. Sam watched them for a moment and then turned to look out at the lake. The play of sunlight on the waves seemed to tease him…to beckon him. Sean had loved the lake. They had enjoyed so many good times on this beach that he couldn't help feeling some of that remembered joy. His throat tightened when it hit him that he would never have another perfect summer day on the beach with his son. His jaw tensed and he blinked hard before he took three running steps and dove under the water in an attempt to wash away the agony. The clear cool water closed over his head, and he opened his eyes a tiny bit as he glided along a foot above the lake bed. Sunlight cut through the water, reflecting off the sand beneath him, and making a few stones sparkle like diamonds. His lungs felt about to burst but held out as long as he could. Down here, it was as though a part of his son was with him again. He surfaced with a shake of his head. After swiping water from his eyes, he found Molly watching him, her lips curved into a smile.

An hour later, Sam left the two so he could do some laps between his pier, and the one fifty yards away in front of the neighbor's home. Swimming had always relaxed him, the rhythm almost hypnotizing as he had to concentrate on the strokes and when to take a breath. The motion tugged at the tape holding his wound together, but the heat and the water had loosened the muscles. He hadn't realized how much he missed swimming. He missed the control. For the last two years, first with his undercover work, and then after the fire, he'd felt like his whole life had been out of his control, but today, he'd taken the first steps toward regaining it.

Sam swam at a steady pace and allowed his mind to work on the problem of Johnny and his entanglement with the Ravens. When Sam had planned his own revenge on Howard, he hadn't counted on anyone else being involved in his plan to exact justice from Howard, only now Johnny was smack dab in the middle of it. For the last year, Sam had been assigned minor cases—the same level he had been assigned when he had first become an ATF agent. He had been told it was for his own safety until they had Howard in custody, but Sam suspected they didn't trust him anymore. Last month he had confronted his boss, and demanded to be reassigned—to be allowed to track down Howard, but his demand was denied. They said someone else was working on it. With that, Sam tendered his resignation. His boss hadn't accepted it. At least, not yet. He insisted that Sam take a month and maybe he would feel differently. Sam had grudgingly complied, but he had no intention of changing his mind, just his plan. Since it seemed nobody was interested in bringing Howard to justice, Sam planned to exact his own vengeance. With no family left, he had no reason to be cautious and when he finally found Howard, he planned to be judge, jury and executioner all in one.

At the end of his second round trip between the dock on his property and the next one, about fifty yards away, Sam held onto the piling and caught his breath. A speedboat zipped across the lake, and farther out, a small sailboat skimmed the surface. He should take his boat out of storage. Kelsie would probably love to go for a ride. He made a mental note to take a look at it. One of the neighbors had taken care of pulling it off the lake last fall and winterizing it. It wasn't a fancy boat, but it had a big enough engine to tow a water skier.

He was in his home territory. It would be hard for the Ravens to find them here. The house was set back from the road and didn't have a house number. Any mail went to a P.O box in town. The Northwoods were dotted with small towns like his, and there were dozens of small lakes surrounding the town.

Outsiders had a hard time finding their way through the winding forest roads. Some roads cut between lakes, then circled one lake before branching off to encompass another lake. It all looked the same. Sam counted on that to help keep them safe.

Done with his swim, he slogged through the shallow water and caught his breath at the sight of Molly stretched out on the other Adirondack chair, her ankles crossed. Sunglasses hid her eyes, but he knew she was awake since Kelsie still played on the water's edge. He felt her gaze on him even through the glasses. His heart rate, already fast after his swim, sped up as she watched him cross to the other chair. He grabbed his towel and swiped his face and chest before sitting on the end of the lounger. Molly's lounger angled so the foot of it almost touched the foot of his. Hot pink nail color decorated her toenails.

"How was the swim?"

"Huh?" He swallowed hard and tore his gaze from her delicate feet, only to slide it up her lightly tanned legs that seemed miles long. Toned and trim, she had the legs of a runner or bicyclist. When his gaze finally made it to her face, she had her head cocked, one eyebrow visible above the rim of the glasses a smile parting her lips. "Oh. It was good. Real good." He drew his shoulders back to work out a kink in his back.

"Is your back sore?"

"Just a little."

"Here, let me take a look at your wound." She scooted to the end of the chair and motioned for him to turn his back towards her. "The steri-strips are starting to peel, but that's okay as long as the skin is healing."

He couldn't suppress the shiver that shook him as her fingers traced along his back and a groan escaped when one fingernail lightly scratched him.

"Oh! I'm so sorry! Did I hurt you? I was trying to make the tape stick again." Her hands ran up to his shoulders as she turned him to face her again.

It hadn't been a groan of pain, but embarrassed, he shrugged and then winced as the movement pulled at his sore muscles. "Forget it."

"Here, allow me." Her hands felt warm and soft against his water-cooled skin as she kneaded the base of his neck.

If she was trying to relax him, her method wasn't working. He tensed, every nerve attuned to her touch. He wanted her to stop before he lost control, but at the same time, he never wanted her to stop.

"Sam? Relax. Jeez, you're so stiff!"

That did it. He burst out laughing. He couldn't help it. The tension drained right out of him as he bent over in another wave of laughter.

Molly giggled and when he straightened to wipe tears out of his eyes, he grinned at her.

She bit her lip, her face flushing a deep red. "That came out wrong."

He hadn't laughed like that in a long time. It felt good. It felt better than good. It felt fantastic. Their faces were only inches apart and he reached out, cupping the back of her head and leaned in, brushing her lips with his.

The scent of sunscreen, sand and sun filled his nose. She made a small sound in her throat as the kiss deepened. He steadied her with his other arm around her waist, his hand resting on her bare skin.

"Mommy?"

Sam tore his mouth away as Molly pushed against his chest. Her breath came in short gasps as she turned to Kelsie. "Yes, honey?"

"What are you doing? Did Mr. Sam drown?" Her little face pinched in concern.

Molly shot a startled glance at Sam before turning back to Kelsie. "No. Sam's fine. Why would you think he drowned?"

"Cause that's what you do when someone drowns. You breathe into them."

"You are so smart, Kels! Where did you learn that?"

Sam bit back a grin and mumbled out of the side of his mouth, "Nice re-direct."

He stood and held out his hand to Kelsie. "Why don't we go inside and see if your Uncle Johnny is still sleeping? Then maybe we can have a little cookout. How does that sound?"

"Can we roast marshmallows?" She put her hand in his without hesitation and they headed back to the house.

"Absolutely." He smiled down at her. "We might even have the makings of S'mores."

Her eyes grew huge and it was all he could do not to sweep her into a hug.

Molly caught up to them, the bucket and shovel that Kelsie had been playing with dangling from her hand. "Talk about *me* redirecting..."

Sam winked at her.

As they reached the house, he heard the grind of gravel from a car turning into the drive. He froze and held out his arm, blocking Molly's way. "Listen up. Wait here until I see who it is. If it's okay, I'll be back in a second. If I'm not right back, take Kelsie to that third cabin, the one that borders the woods."

Molly's eyes widened as she nodded. With a glance towards the sound of a door slamming, she took Kelsie's hand and went down on one knee, whispering into the little girl's ear.

CHAPTER SIX

Sam took a deep breath and rounded the corner, wishing he hadn't left his gun in the house. Just because he was home didn't make them safe. Footsteps sounded on the wooden steps up to the porch. They sounded too light for a man. From his vantage point on the side of the house, he could see the car. A maroon Ford Explorer with Wisconsin plates. At least it wasn't a motorcycle.

A knock rattled the screen door.

Sam eased around the corner and glanced into the vehicle as he passed it. A large red bag lay carelessly on the front seat. Victoria's bag.

Relief swept him. Since she hadn't seen him yet, he ducked back around the house and motioned for Molly.

"Just Victoria. Come on."

Molly looked relieved, but rolled her eyes. "Does she have a tracking device on you or what?"

Sam laughed and said, "Oh come on, it's only the second time we've seen her."

Molly's eyebrow quirked, but she didn't say anything as they turned the corner.

Victoria stepped down the stairs, her feet encased in impossibly high sandals and she wore the tiniest pair of white shorts Sam had ever seen. They set off her tan very well, but she had the look of a woman trying too hard. The skimpy tank top completed the picture.

"Well, there you guys are. I just knocked and nobody answered." She put her hands on her hips and pouted as if she'd been stood up.

"Hello, Victoria. We were on the beach." That fact should have been obvious considering their attire, but Sam doubted Victoria noticed.

"Hello...again." Molly wore a smile, but it didn't reach her eyes. He was sure Victoria wouldn't notice that either.

Victoria nodded to Molly, but she won a point when she grinned at Kelsie. "Hi again, sugar. You're just the cutest thing in that little swimsuit."

"So, Victoria, is there something you needed?" Time to cut to the chase.

She turned from the child. "Well, I was just at a friend's house up the road, and since I was in the area, I thought I'd stop by. I was feeling nostalgic." She smiled and stepped closer to Sam. "Remember when we were kids and we used to just run into each other's houses all the time? You practically lived at our cabin that one summer."

"Yeah, I did. By the way, how is Tony doing? Your brother and I lost touch with each other." Victoria made it sound like he'd been there to see her instead of hanging out with her brother, Dave. Sam had barely noticed Victoria, who'd been four years younger than Sam.

"Well, if you two will excuse us, it sounds like you have some catching up to do." Molly brushed sand off Kelsie's shoulder. "Come on, sweetie, let's get you into a bath. You have sand everywhere."

Sam called after Molly, "I'll get the grill going."

"Grill? You're having a cook-out?"

The hopeful look in Victoria's eyes pushed him to offer, "Not really, just some burgers, but you're welcome to stay."

She beamed. "I'd love to."

Damn. Before he could say anything more, Johnny stepped onto the porch.

"Molly wanted to know if you need charcoal or if it's a gas—" The poor guy almost stepped on his tongue when he caught sight of Victoria.

Sam could almost hear it snap back like a tape measure retracting as Johnny took the steps in one bound and was beside Victoria. He stuck out his hand. "Hi. I'm Johnny Flynn."

Victoria smiled and took his hand. "Victoria Matlock. " Her head cocked to the side. "Flynn? Are you Molly's husband?"

Johnny laughed. "Oh god, no. She's my sister."

"Ah, now I see the resemblance."

"You're going to stay and eat with us, right?" Johnny touched her arm and motioned to the porch. "We have plenty."

Apparently enjoying the worship in Johnny's eyes, Victoria's voice dropped a notch and she smiled coyly. "Yes, Sam has invited me. I was going to say no, but now that I've met you, I think I'd love to stay."

Johnny's chest puffed up and Sam wanted to gag. Instead, he pushed between them. "Excuse me, I need to start the grill."

"Oh my heavens, Sam! What happened to your back?"

He turned at the top of the steps and shook his head. "It's nothing. A little accident."

"Poor baby! It must have hurt." Victoria's brow furrowed in concern, and at least that emotion looked genuine.

Sam waved his hands. "Nah, it's fine. Why don't you two sit on the porch and get to know each other?"

"Can't you sit with us?"

Johnny scowled at him and it was all Sam could do not to laugh. "Sorry, if we're going to eat tonight, I have to the grill going, but talk to Johnny. He's a *fascinating* guy."

Victoria pouted, but then smiled at Johnny. "I'm sure he is."

Sam escaped into the house and into the kitchen, thankful when Victoria didn't follow him. He sorted through their grocery bags and found the small bag of charcoal, and paused in the hallway, warmed by the giggles that came from the bathroom.

After starting the grill, he returned to the kitchen and washed his hands. Molly stood at the counter rolling balls of hamburger and smashing them into patties. She didn't speak to him and he knew his next comment probably wouldn't go over well, but he stepped behind her and slid his hands around her waist. She had showered and wore a soft pink t-shirt and cut-offs. Her hair was still damp and pulled into a ponytail. He pulled her close and nuzzled the back of her neck.

A shiver shook her, so he knew she wasn't immune, but she tried to shrug him off. "I'm busy, Sam."

"Yes, I see that. Um…could you make sure there's enough for five?"

She tilted her head back to glance up at him. "Five?" A meat patty slapped against the wax paper she'd spread on the counter as she dropped it. "You invited *her*?" Her nose wrinkled in distaste, then she scraped up the patty and re-shaped it. It joined a stack already on a tray.

"I did. What was I going to do? Just stand there after she asked if we were having a cookout?"

He couldn't see her roll her eyes, but he was sure she did. He felt it in her stiff posture. With a lift of one shoulder, she shook her head. "I suppose not, and it's your house. Sorry I said anything. It's none of my business who you want over for dinner."

Sam applied light pressure against the right side of her abdomen, urging her to turn towards him. She resisted for a few seconds, then twisted to face him, one eyebrow raised, her hands held out to her side so as not to touch him.

"Don't worry about her. Her brother was my best friend, but she was just the kid sister who bugged us. From what I can tell, she hasn't changed much." He grinned. "Besides, I think your brother caught her eye," Sam added, hoping to ease her mind.

Molly shot a look towards the porch. "You don't have to explain your actions. It's not like what happened last night can ever happen again."

Sam stepped back in surprise. "What do you mean?" He hoped the kiss on the beach had meant something, but she had already warned him this morning that they didn't have a future. In the heat of the moment, he had forgotten. Damn it.

Molly turned and resumed forming the hamburgers. "I told you. I can't get involved with someone right now. I have my daughter to think about."

"I understand—I really do, but just so you know, I would never in a million years do anything to hurt Kelsie."

Molly nodded. "I know you wouldn't mean to. I can see how good you are with her, but we have a life back home and the sooner we get back to it, the better. Before Kelsie gets too attached."

The ache in his chest caught him by surprise. For a little while, the pain he'd lived with for the last year had dampened, but it came back full-force at her statement. Without a word, he left the kitchen.

* * *

Molly bit her lip as Sam's footsteps retreated, telling herself that being honest with Sam was the right thing to do. The situation was too volatile. It was bad enough she and Kelsie had to leave their home, even if it was due to her brother and not

Sam. She couldn't let her daughter become too attached to a man who would walk out of their lives when the situation changed.

After the burgers were ready to be cooked, she opened a package of frozen corn and poured it into a pan, setting it on the stove ready to heat when the hamburgers were close to being done. Molly pulled the potato salad out of the fridge along with the makings for a tossed salad. There wasn't anything more to do right now and she admitted to herself that she was stalling. She didn't want to face Sam or make small talk with Victoria. Kelsie had gone out to the porch, not wanting to miss anything.

Chin high, she took the platter of burgers, along with a clean one for the cooked meat, and headed out to Sam. The grill was on a cement apron at the side of the drive and she had to walk past Johnny and Victoria to reach it. She nodded and smiled, hoping it looked more genuine than it felt. Sam took the platter with a quiet thank you, his face impassive.

She looked around, wondering what to do next. Johnny and Victoria were deep in conversation, Sam wasn't speaking to her, and Kelsie was playing with a couple of stuffed animals at the far end of the porch.

With a sigh, she sat on the steps. It was too nice of an evening to sit cooped up inside the house. The hamburgers sizzled on the grill, and as the scent wafted past, her stomach growled. The hours on the beach had whet her appetite. Sam had changed out of his swimming trunks and wore a gray t-shirt and an old worn pair of jeans.

"Hey, Sam?"

He glanced over his shoulder. "Yes?"

She winced at his impersonal tone, but she had it coming. "I should probably take a look at your wounds."

He didn't face her, just flipped a couple of burgers. "They're fine. I can take care of them."

"Oh. Okay. Well, let me know if you need any help."

"I won't."

Molly stared at his back for a minute before standing. It was probably better that he was angry with her. It would make it easier for them to stay away from each other. The reasoning didn't help ease the sting as she climbed the steps to the porch.

"Molly?"

She paused at the top of the steps, and faced him.

"Thank you for what you've done. I know I should have thanked you sooner, and I apologize for my thoughtlessness. You've been wonderful through all this." He held her gaze for a long moment before he gave a quick nod and turned back to the grill.

"You're welcome, Sam." She didn't know if he heard her, but didn't wait to find out as she hurried into the house to hide the tears welling in her eyes. If he'd have been a jerk about it, it would be a lot easier, but no, he had to go and be all civil to her.

A few minutes later, they all sat down to eat, and Molly was actually thankful for the buffer of Victoria. Between her and Kelsie, they kept up a steady stream of chatter. Sam asked Victoria about a few people they both had known, and Johnny questioned Victoria about where people went to have fun up here. Molly ate her dinner, barely tasting a thing, and admonished Kelsie to talk a little less and eat a little more.

After they ate and cleaned up the kitchen, Kelsie reminded Sam about his promise of S'mores. Sam looked at Molly for permission before agreeing to making the treat. She was bone-tired, but Kelsie had such a look of hope on her face, she couldn't crush it. "I'll get the stuff together. You guys find the sticks for the marshmallows."

Sam rested his hand on the top of Kelsie's head and bent to hear whatever it was she was saying as the two left the kitchen. It had been only a few days, but already her daughter was completely smitten with Sam. Molly couldn't blame her. He was hard to resist.

After gathering the chocolate, marshmallows and graham crackers, Molly approached the living room, intending to ask if Johnny and Victoria wanted to join them in making the treats, but she paused before entering when she heard Sam's name mentioned. She peeked in to find Victoria and Johnny sitting on the couch looking at a book.

Curious, she crossed to them. "What's that?"

They jumped, and Victoria started to close the book, but then she giggled. "Just a photo album. I was showing Johnny some pictures from when Sam, my brother and I all hung out together."

She flipped through a few pages. "Oh, look, there he is in his uniform. You should have seen him, Molly. He was so handsome!"

Johnny scowled, but Victoria gave him a playful slap on the thigh. "That was ages ago, Johnny."

"Oh! And look, here's one of little Sean! I only saw him a few times in town, but he was just the most adorable little boy. It's so sad." Victoria patted the cushion beside her. "Come and look, Molly."

Molly wanted to see, but held back. She had no right to spy into Sam's past, but it was just a photograph and he'd told her about Sean. Her curiosity won out over her reluctance and she leaned sideways to see the photo.

Sean had one arm around his dad's neck as Sam knelt beside him. The snapshot had been taken on the pier she'd seen down at the lake. The little boy held up a small fish and beamed at the camera. Sam's pride and love was evident in the way he looked not at the camera, but at Sean, his hand resting on top of his son's head.

The screen door slammed and Molly turned just as Sam strode past her, his hand held out to Victoria. "Give me that."

Victoria shrugged and gave it to him. "Sorry. I didn't think you'd mind. After all, the album was on the mantle. It wasn't like I went snooping around for it."

A muscle jumped in Sam's jaw, but he simply nodded. His gaze shifted to Molly and his face unreadable as he said, "Kelsie found some sticks."

"Okay. Thanks." She slipped past him, unable to look him in the eye. A few minutes later, she tried her best to put on a good front for Kelsie. Thankfully, the little girl was having too much fun roasting marshmallows and sandwiching them between chocolate and graham crackers to notice how distracted Molly was acting. Sam had walked around the side of the house and she supposed he was probably at the beach.

Just as Kelsie squished the third S'more together, Sam stepped onto the porch. He glanced at Molly, but when Kelsie presented him with the S'more, his stony facade cracked.

"You made one for me?"

"Well, duh!" Kelsie snickered. "Of course we did, silly."

Sam accepted it and Kelsie watched him as if she was expecting to win a blue ribbon for her culinary skills. Sam took a bite. Crumbs fell onto his shirt, and marshmallow stuck to the corner of his mouth. "Mmm...mmm. This is the best one I've had in a very long time, Kelsie."

Kelsie glowed. Molly could have kissed him for his reply.

"Where's your's?" Sam pointed to Molly's empty hands.

"I thought that one was mine, but my daughter sold me out."

Sam winked at Kelsie and said to Molly, "Kelsie and I have an agreement when it comes to stuff like this. She gives me first dibs, and I do the same for her."

Molly crossed her arms in mock anger. "Oh, you do, do you?"

Kelsie had already poked another marshmallow onto the end of a stick, and held it over the fire. "Don't worry, Mommy, you can have this one."

For another twenty minutes, they ate S'mores, keeping the banter light. After they finished up, Molly tucked Kelsie in bed. The sun was just setting and even though it was close to ten 'o'clock, it just didn't seem late enough to go to bed yet.

The house was quiet and she wondered where the others had gone. She headed to the porch and stood with hands partially jammed into her front jean pockets. Sam was stirring the coals, scattering them in the grill. Shoving her hands into her back pockets, she glanced around. Victoria's car was gone. "Did Johnny go to bed?"

Sam shook his head. "No. He and Victoria went to a bar."

Molly rolled her eyes. "Figures."

Sam rolled the grill away from the house, and dusted his hands on his jeans. "Yeah. I advised him to stay here tonight, but short of telling the whole story in front of Victoria, there wasn't much I could say. At least she's driving." He opened the porch door and Molly felt a pang of disappointment that he was going in the house, but he only reached his hand inside and a second later, a porch light on the side near the driveway flicked on. Carefully, he closed the door so it wouldn't slam,

"Yeah." Why couldn't Johnny ever listen to anyone? Molly plopped onto the swing and closed her eyes. The woods were alive with the hum of insects and chirping of crickets. Bullfrogs croaked down by the lake adding to the natural symphony. The sounds lulled her into a relaxed state, almost dozing. A few minutes later, the swing jerked and Molly's eyes flew open to find Sam sitting beside her. He'd left a little room, but his knee brushed against hers, sending a spark of heat up her leg.

Sam studied her face for moment. "I'm sorry."

"For what?"

"For how I acted about the photo album."

Molly lifted one shoulder. "We were being nosy. There's no need to apologize."

"Yes, there is. I haven't been able to look at the album since he died, but that's *my* problem. You weren't doing anything wrong."

Unable to think of a reply, Molly simply nodded. Sam slid down a bit, resting his head against the wall behind the swing, his legs stretched out in front of him. His knee no longer touched hers and she missed it. It was just proof that she had made the right decision. It would be a lot less painful for all involved that the relationship ended sooner rather than later. She was sure the pain would ease quickly—after all, they had only known each other for less than a week. True relationships needed longer than that to develop. A yawn overtook her. Last night's flight from home and today's time on the beach had caught up to her and she could barely keep her eyes open. She was sure that fatigue was the major cause of her doubts as to whether she'd made the right decision. By morning, she would be glad she had put a halt to things.

* * *

"Do you want another?" Molly held a pancake-laden spatula poised over Sam's plate waiting for him to reply. He nodded and she slipped it onto the pile of three already stacked on his dish. It had been almost a week since they had arrived and tensions were strained between them. Sam had taken to sleeping in his son's old room so that she and Kelsie could have the larger bed. The last few days, Sam had left for most of the day, returning in the evenings. He didn't say where he was going, but she had an idea that he was taking road trips back to her town or that area. It would explain his fatigue when he returned every evening. With that many hours on the road, plus whatever he did in between, she didn't know how he was managing to function.

"Thanks for making breakfast. I appreciate it." Sam dug into the pile. Stubble dotted his jaw. More than a day's growth so he was either too tired to shave or wanted to change his appearance. She was betting on the latter.

"I'd have made breakfast for you yesterday, but you were gone when I woke up." She put the last three pancakes on her own plate and sat to eat. Kelsie had already eaten her breakfast and was playing on the porch. "I'm trying not to be nosy, but since I've had my life turned upside down, I decided I had a right to know what's going on. Where do you go every day?"

"Out. Going town to town asking at biker bars about the Ravens."

"Why? Aren't we supposed to be hiding from them?"

"You, Kelsie and Johnny are hiding from them." He took a drink of milk and shrugged. "I don't want to sit around waiting for them to track your brother down, so I've taken the offensive."

"What does that mean, exactly?"

"I don't want to be ambushed by them, so want to know where they are. So far, I've come up empty. I've hit some of their old hangouts that I knew from last year, but it's summertime and they're probably making the bike rally rounds."

"You know, you don't have to rush home at night if your travels take you far away."

"I don't want to leave you and Kelsie alone at night. It's a long shot that they'd come here, but just in case."

"Johnny's here, and I have my car most of the time since he's out with Victoria."

"I know you would rather that I was gone, but I don't trust your brother to protect you and like you said, he's usually not even here at night." He spoke matter of fact, but it still stung when he said it—as if Molly hated him or something.

"That's not it, Sam. It's just that you look exhausted. I thought you could get a lot more rest if you stayed at a hotel instead of driving back here every night." The pancake felt leaden in her stomach after the second bite. Not for the first time she wondered why she had to meet Sam under these circumstances. Why did there have to be so many complications? She poked her fork into another bit of pancake, but couldn't work up the energy to bring it to her mouth. She laid the fork down with a sigh. "Your idea that we don't want you around couldn't be further from the truth. Kelsie asks about you every day."

His eyes softened. "She does?"

Molly nodded and spread her hands. "This place is wonderful, but when you're not here, it feels empty—like it's missing something." Embarrassed at the disclosure, she stood and gathered Kelsie's dirty plate along with her own, and put them in the sink. Behind her, Sam continued eating while she washed the dishes.

A few minutes later, he stood behind her and reached around, slipping his own dishes into the sink. "I was thinking of taking a few days off. You're right. I'm worn out and so far, I've come up with nothing."

Molly grinned down at the dish in her hand and took the bottle of dish soap, squeezing a drop on the plate. A flurry of bubbles escaped from the bottle, floating and sparkling in the sunlight streaming into the kitchen. "Kelsie will be thrilled."

The heat from his body enveloped her as he moved even closer, and she looked over her shoulder to find his face only inches away. His eyes searched hers. "What about you?"

Flustered at his nearness, she stuttered, "I...I'm okay with it."

His eyes warmed, crinkling in the corners, but he didn't smile. "Just okay with it?"

She shrugged, unable to drag her gaze from his.

His hand came up and she leaned towards the caress, but it never came. Instead, he brushed his fingers across a few of her curls. "You had a couple of bubbles clinging."

Then he turned away and ambled out of the kitchen.

* * *

Molly loved the cabin and the beach, but she was getting stir crazy and when she said something about it, Sam suggested they go for a ride. The three of them drove the winding roads through the forest. It took them by several other lakes and Molly marveled at some of the huge summer homes but her favorites were the small cozy cottages. "The lakes are so beautiful, I might have to look for a job up here after I finish school. I bet I could buy a nice little cottage like one of those, don't you think?"

"Winters can get pretty bad."

Molly waved that off. "Eh, I have four-wheel drive. Maybe I'll get a snowmobile. I've only been on one once and it was a blast. Do you snowmobile?"

Sam nodded. "Not in a long time, but there's a snowmobile in the shed. Like the boat, it would need some tuning up, but it's in running condition."

"Wow, you have everything up here." Molly grinned at Sam. "I can't imagine why you ever left."

A shadow crossed Sam's face as he shrugged. "I've been asking myself that question a lot lately."

After awhile they wound up on the highway and Sam took them to town. Molly and Kelsie explored several gift shops.

Molly bought a few books for herself from the small selection one shop carried, and purchased a couple of Barbie dolls for Kelsie. Afterward, they ate dinner at a restaurant decorated with stuffed deer heads.

"Are they alive?" Kelsie stared at the creatures, her eyes huge. "They look so real!"

Sam glanced at the trophies and grinned. "No, they're not alive anymore."

Turning her gaze onto Sam, Kelsie asked in a hushed tone, "*Anymore*?"

"Uh, Kels, how about some chicken tenders?" She needed to distract her daughter from the deer. The reality of the deer's fate was a little much for a six year old to handle.

Back at the house, Kelsie played in the living room with her new dolls. Restless, Molly headed out to the porch, intending to read one of her new books, but she couldn't keep her mind on it. Sam had gone to putter around on the boat, and Johnny was gone, as usual. She barely saw him lately as he spent most evenings out with Victoria.

Sam rounded the corner of the house and headed inside, his hands black with grease. A few minutes later, he came out with a couple of bottles of beer, and offered her one.

Taking it, she set her book aside and scooted over, making room for him to sit on the swing too, if he wanted. "I should go in and check on Kelsie." But she made no move to rise.

The swing creaked as he sat. "No need. She fell asleep on the sofa, a doll clutched in each hand. I covered her with a blanket. She's fine for now."

"Thank you."

He shrugged and took a sip of his beer. "It was a good day I'm glad you convinced me to stay home today."

Molly sighed. It would be so nice to be able to enjoy this without the threat of the Ravens finding them. "Do you really think the motorcycle gang is still after Johnny after all this time? They must have moved on by now."

Sam shook his head. "These gangs don't move on when money is involved. Your brother was in charge of thousands of dollars-worth of drugs. Since it was all confiscated, the gang is out both the drugs and the money. That tends to make them angry."

"But they must know that's a risk they take and that it's not Johnny's fault." Molly wished she could talk to the enforcer guy. See if she could talk sense into him. The gang threatening her brother wasn't going to make him suddenly produce either the drugs or the money. It was stupid. They were stupid. She slapped a mosquito that landed on her arm. It was getting towards dusk and a few were buzzing around. A steady breeze kept most away though.

"I agree but they don't think like you or I think. If they did, they wouldn't do what they do. Most of them are psychopaths and don't care about anyone except themselves." He nodded towards her arm. "Killing someone causes them about as much remorse as you felt after smacking that mosquito."

Molly looked at where she'd squashed the mosquito and tried to muster up a smidgen of guilt, but it wouldn't come. "It's just a mosquito—you can't compare it to a person."

Sam shrugged. "That's exactly how they think about other people. If that person isn't important to them, they don't have any value."

She thought about his comparison and found it hard to accept, but Sam should know. After all, the gang had murdered his son and mother. The fact that the same people were after Johnny made her blood run cold. "If you find them first, will you arrest them? That'll save Johnny."

Sam turned to her, his expression intense. "I can't arrest them without evidence. I don't have it where my son is concerned and I certainly don't have it in Johnny's case. No, I plan to exact my own justice."

He broke eye contact and stared across the yard, apparently lost in thought, she gave his knee a shake. "Sam...What exactly do you mean by justice? Why can't you dig up more evidence and arrest him?"

Sam turned to her, his eyes still far away before they cleared and filled with anger. "Arrest wasn't what I had in mind. I've taken a leave of absence from the ATF, remember?"

"If not arrest, then...what?"

He tilted his head and said, his voice low and hard, "Don't make me say it, Molly. What would *you* do if it happened to Kelsie?"

Just the mention of something happening to her daughter sent a shiver through her. She would want to kill the bastard. It was a gut reaction. "Listen, Sam. I know I'd want to do what...what you're implying, but it wouldn't bring her back, and I'd just end up in prison for murder."

Sam shrugged. "After I make him pay, I don't care what happens to me."

"What about your friends? I'm sure they'd care."

"Didn't have many, and the few I had, I drove off over the last year."

She tried to hide the hurt, tugging the sheet even higher. "I know it's only been a few days, but I consider you a friend now. *More* than a friend."

He glanced at her, but immediately looked away, the muscle in his jaw flexing. After several strained moments of silence, he said, "You shouldn't consider me a friend. I'm more like a cloud of death that envelopes everyone I care about."

Molly latched onto the last part. "So does that mean you care about me?"

He bent, knees wide elbows propped on them as he cradled his head in his hands. "I'm sorry. I never meant for this to happen. My plan was supposed to involve just me and the enforcer. Now I've gone and dragged you into it." With his face buried in his hands, it came out muffled.

Molly shook her head even though he couldn't see it. She stood and paused before him. "You didn't drag us into it, remember? That was my brother's doing. Those Ravens would have chased Johnny to my house whether you were there or not. Only if you hadn't been there, who knows how it might have turned out?"

He dragged his hands down his face and sighed as he straightened. "That may be true but if you stay with me, you *will* be in the middle of it."

"But we're safe here. Nobody knows where we are."

Sam nodded, but said, "That's the case now, but it's only a matter of time before they track Johnny down. The night we came up here I waited for the two who were chasing us and I sent a message that I'd exact my revenge. However, I offered to let it go if the enforcer considers Johnny's debt paid in full."

"You'd do that for Johnny? Give up all plans of revenge?" The hope in her eyes cut into him.

"I would, but I don't think Howard will go for it. He's not one to accept someone else's terms. At the very least, I still have to find him and convince him that it's in his best interest to accept the deal."

"I appreciate that you're taking on Johnny's problems, but what am I supposed to do, Sam? If they can find us here, why not just go back home?" Molly paced to the porch railing and peered into the encroaching darkness. Were they out there even now?

Sam shook his head. "No. You're right that nobody knows where you are, but Johnny and I need to leave to make sure they don't find you."

"Leave? Where do I go?"

"Nowhere. You and Kelsie can stay here." Sam rose and took her by the shoulders. "It's the only solution. You and Kelsie can stay here as long as necessary. As long as Johnny isn't here, you'll be safe. They wouldn't make the connection. Maybe we'll go back to your place and scout around, see if they were there at all."

"What about my job? Kelsie's on summer break, but I only have a couple of weeks of vacation. I can't afford to lose my job, Sam. I have bills to pay." Anger coursed through her. Her whole life had unraveled through no fault of her own.

"Molly, I don't think you get it. You can't go back there. Not now. Maybe not for a long time. The gang knows the house, and by now, they've probably combed through everything in it and know more about you than you want to know."

"So that's it? I'm just done as a paramedic?"

"I have money, Molly. I'll make sure you have everything you need." Sam rose and crossed to her. "Do you need something now?" He reached for his wallet, but Molly shook her head.

"It's not about money. I love being a paramedic."

"And you're a damned good one, I know that first hand, but for the near future, you'll have to lay low." He brushed her hair from her face, his thumb caressing her jaw. "I'm sorry. When this is all over, we can straighten everything out."

His touch ignited the feelings she'd been trying to suppress and she pushed past him and returned to the swing. "I just want it to be over soon. I feel like my life is on hold."

"That's how I've felt for a year."

They sat in silence, listening to the crickets chirping, and the croaking of the frogs down in the lake. Her temple still tingled where Sam's fingers had grazed her skin. She'd lied when she had said her life was on hold. As soon as she'd said it, she realized that with the exception of her daughter, nothing in her life mattered to her as much as Sam.

Without thinking, she scooted close to him until their thighs bumped. He rolled his head to look at her, an eyebrow raised in question.

Feeling heat climb her face, she was thankful for the dark. "Maybe I was too quick with my decision."

"Decision?"

"Yeah, you know…about our relationship."

He was quiet for so long she wondered if he was ignoring her, but finally he said, "I know it's only been a few days, but under the circumstances, it feels as if I've known you longer, but at the same time I don't really know you at all."

"There's not much to know. I've already told you that I work part-time as a paramedic and I'm working to complete my degree, but my semester just ended. I'm taking the summer off to be with my daughter as much as I can. As you can see, I'm a single mom, so that doesn't leave me much time to socialize. If you're looking for excitement, you might want to keep looking." Molly chuckled. "Well, that is, except for my brother. He's doing his best to liven things up."

Sam smiled. "Yeah, he is at that." The porch was dark and shadowed now, but her eyes had become accustomed to it and a pensive look crossed his face. "I don't want to seem nosy, but where is Kelsie's father?"

"Do you mean, is he in the picture?" He nodded. Molly bit her lip and averted her gaze. Should she tell him? It really wasn't any of his business and with his history with the Ravens, he might have even met Kelsie's sperm donor. That's how Molly always thought of him—he didn't deserve to be called a father and certainly not a dad. She hated to lie, but then she ran the question he had asked over in her mind. He hadn't asked who Kelsie's father was, just if he was in the picture. Relieved that she could be completely truthful, she explained, "He saw her once when she was a month old but never wanted anything to do with her. The last few years, Kelsie's been asking more questions about her father and I hate that I don't have any good answers for her. How do you tell a little girl that her daddy is basically nothing but a few strands of DNA?" Molly crossed her arms and didn't wait for Sam to reply. "I've run out of excuses to give her so I just tell her that her dad lives far away, but he loves her very much."

Sam shook his head. "He's missing out. I'd give anything..." He blinked a few times, the muscles in his jaw clenching as he turned his head away.

Reaching over she rested her hand on his knee, giving it a gentle squeeze while a lump formed in her throat.

He shifted, his gaze fixed on the woods across the road. Fireflies flickered in the blackness, and she didn't think she had ever seen so many at one time before.

After a long moment, Sam cleared his throat and said, "I'm not looking for excitement. I've had my fill of that." He glanced around and made a vague gesture towards the house. "I loved this place when I was a kid. I always wanted to live here, but we could only stay in the summer. It was my grandparents' cabin and they lived here in the summers and went to Florida in the winters. I would come up after school let out for the summer and my parents would come up most weekends. The best times were when we were all here together. We had bonfires on the beach at least once a week and I loved fishing with my dad early in the mornings. I begged them to move up here, but..." He sighed and shrugged. "They had their jobs. I didn't understand it when I was a kid, but I had the same excuse for Sean. My grandparents died before Sean was born and my father when Sean was an infant. My mom almost sold the house then. There was just my mom and I at that point and we didn't come up here very often. It was a lot of work to maintain when nobody was living here, but she just didn't have the heart to sell it. When Sean was old enough, we started spending a few weeks here again. It wasn't much, but those were the best times I ever spent with my son. Sometimes we would come up at Christmas, too. It's really beautiful with all the snow."

Molly nodded. "I can imagine." After a pause, she asked, "So, are you planning on selling the house now?" Immediately, she regretted her question. It was thoughtless and what business was it of hers? He gave her a quick glance, but in the dark, she couldn't read his expression and he turned forward again without answering.

She studied his profile, highlighted by the soft yellow porch light. He had a strong brow, a straight nose that fit his face perfectly. She envied his high cheekbones and lips made masculine by a hint of five o'clock shadow. Kissing him was a contrast in textures with soft but firm lips and sandpapery whiskers that led to a chin with the hint of a cleft. If she could, she would stamp the image in her mind—imprint it forever— and wish they had met at different times in their lives.

He finally spoke, his voice low and husky, "I don't know. I just don't know."

They settled into silence with only the sounds of the forest breaking the stillness. After several minutes, Molly said, "I hope you keep it."

The swing creaked as Sam moved, shifting to look at her. "Why?" He sounded surprised.

Shrugging, Molly slapped her arm as she felt the sting of a mosquito. She waited a beat for guilt to kick in, but it still didn't come, and she doubted it ever would. "I always want to picture you up here. It feels like you belong in these woods and this cottage. I didn't know you before…before everything happened, and it probably sounds silly, but I can feel the love in this house." Embarrassed, she stood and stepped to the porch railing again.

The swing thumped lightly against the front of the house as he rose and moved to her side. "I can't live here for the same reason my parents couldn't. It's not where my job is located."

"Are you still in the ATF? I know you said you're on leave, but…" She hadn't been sure when he explained but then wondered if he was allowed to reveal his status with the government agency. "I'm sorry. I seem to keep asking questions I have no right to ask."

Sam chuckled. "You're fine. Yes, I'm on leave and I'm not supposed to be doing what I'm doing, but that didn't matter to me." He leaned both hands on the railing and shrugged. "I never thought beyond getting revenge."

"But now you're going to just arrest him, right?

He grunted. "Yeah, but sadly, inside of a day he'd be out on bail and disappear. I've seen it happen before. I know it's not what you want, but I can't see any other solution but to take Howard down."

Molly caught her breath as cold invaded her body as if someone had dipped her in a vat of ice water. Howard? She backed up a step, bumping into the corner of the railing. No, it couldn't be. Ray was an ass and a jerk, and she still felt shame at how he had tricked her into bed, but he wasn't a killer. He couldn't be the guy Sam kept calling The Enforcer.

"Who is Howard?" She prayed silently that it was a different man with the same last name. It was pretty common, after all.

"Howard…Ray Howard…the Enforcer." Sam regarded her, his head cocked. "Why? Do you know him?" The last was asked in a low, hard voice.

Swallowing hard, Molly gripped the railing behind her, and shook her head. She opened her mouth to tell him yes, but even with his face in shadows, she felt his hostility roll over her. "No…no, I don't think so." Unable to meet his eyes, she ran her hands up and down her arms, and despite the warmth of the evening, she started shivering. "I'm going to go in. It's chilly out here."

Ignoring his questioning look, she brushed past him and went into the house. Unsure where to go, she paused and saw Kelsie snuggled up on the sofa. One doll had slipped from her grasp and lay on the floor. The sweet innocence made a sob catch in her throat. Her daughter could not be related to the man who had killed Sam's son. It couldn't be true. She smoothed the hair back from Kelsie's forehead and pressed a kiss to her brow. Gathering her in her arms, she carried her to bed, hesitating. On one hand, Sam's bed was so much bigger, but she couldn't bear to sleep in his bed. Instead she put Kelsie in Sean's room. Before their trip to town, she had changed all the sheets in the house and put fresh ones on and now she was glad she had. No way could she sleep with Sam's scent enveloping her.

After tucking Kelsie into bed, where the little girl turned over and fell back into a deep sleep, Molly headed to the bathroom. She needed time to think. Why had she lied to Sam? It wasn't as if she felt any loyalty to Ray. Running her hands into her hair, she tried to sort through her emotions. Could Ray have really been behind the death of Sam's son and mother? It was too much to take in. Sitting on the edge of the tub, she cradled her head.

A soft knock sounded on the door. "Molly?"

Molly jumped up and said, "Just a minute."

"I just wondered if you were okay."

"Yeah, I'm fine. I'll be out shortly."

Turning the water on, she stared at herself while waiting for the water to warm. Sam would hate her if he knew. She sobbed, glad for the sound of the running water to cover her sobs. And Kelsie. *Dear God*. He wouldn't even want to look at her. Protectiveness welled inside of her. She had to leave. Kelsie would be disappointed, but she couldn't let Sam's eventual rejection of Kelsie hurt her. She splashed her face with water, scrubbing her eyes. Besides, she was no longer afraid of The Enforcer. Even if he was guilty of what Sam accused him of, she had no fear for herself or for Kelsie anymore. Reaching for the towel on the rack, she patted the water off her face. As evil as Ray could be and might have been, he wouldn't kill his own daughter.

CHAPTER SEVEN

Sam paced the living room. He wanted to believe Molly when she had said she hadn't known Howard but her body language betrayed her. Why had she lied to him and why had she fled his presence?

He replayed their conversation in his mind, stopping at the point where she said he should keep the house. He hadn't considered ever living here, but the last few days, he had felt more alive than he had since Sean's death. Even before his son had died, he had felt disconnected. It was all the undercover work. No matter how hard he tried, he had felt like he was losing himself in the role. The one thing that had anchored him to his real life had been Sean. Sam paused in front of the bookcase and reached for the photo album, pulling it from the slot. Angling the spine across the edge of the mantel, he flipped it open to a random page.

Sean grinned out at him, his little body coated in sand, a blue plastic bucket in one hand and a matching shovel in the other. Beside him was a lump of sand with a few sticks poking out of the top. A castle. Sam's throat ached even as he smiled at the sweet memory of digging in the sand with his son. Blinking hard, he scanned the other photos on the page. Sean holding a tiny fish up, and then another snapshot of him asleep at the dinner table, his cheeks pink from sun, his hand still gripping a fork filled with mashed potatoes. A chuckle squeezed past the ache as Sam recalled taking the picture. Afterward, he had carried Sean to bed. Closing his eyes, he felt again, the warm limp weight of his son against his chest, his head lolling on Sam's shoulder. The memory hurt, but at the same time, joy rose in him. Joy that the memory was so pure and untarnished with thoughts of his son's death. Even though the pain was still there, the joy tempered it.

At the click of the bathroom door opening, Sam shut the album and wiped his forearm across his eyes. Molly padded into the living room, wearing a large t-shirt and soft fleece shorts. It was hardly lingerie, but he knew what was concealed beneath the baggy shirt, and the shorts clung to her curves invitingly. Her face appeared damp, her eyelashes spiky but he attributed it to washing until he noticed a slight red puffiness on her eyelids. She gripped the hem of her shirt, repeatedly twisting it and untwisting it as her gaze darted to the photo album, but other than a slight lift of her eyebrows, she didn't react to it. Instead, she sat on the edge of the recliner opposite him.

"I've decided that Kelsie and I need to go home tomorrow."

Sam gave a shake of his head. "What? You can't. We've already discussed this. As long as your brother is in their radar, they'll stop at nothing to get what they want. If it means using you and Kelsie as bait to get Johnny to cough up the money he owes them, they won't hesitate."

Molly dipped a shoulder and avoided meeting his eyes. "I don't think they will. Why would they come now when they could have done something before?"

"Because they planned on him getting the message when they shot up the bar. Except Johnny didn't have a clue that the message they sent was aimed at him."

Her eyes narrowed. "I know you think Johnny's an idiot, but don't worry, we'll deal with the situation ourselves. We don't need your help."

Setting the album on the coffee table, Sam regarded Molly, unable to hide his surprise at her sudden change of mood. He knew it had something to do with Howard, but since she had denied knowing him, he didn't want to push. He could be wrong about her knowing the man. Molly was just too pure to ever be tarnished by the likes of Howard. He supposed her abrupt change in demeanor had to do with his plan of getting revenge, but she didn't have anything to do with that. Being a paramedic, her job was to save people, not kill them, so it was natural for her to reject Sam's plan, no matter that Howard deserved it. He could certainly respect that view. He used to hold a similar one.

She and Kelsie just needed to stay here so they would be safe from Howard until Sam managed to exact his retribution. Once he had accomplished that, Molly, Kelsie and even Johnny would be safe. Sam would make sure of that even if he had to wrangle them into the Witness Protection program. He had friends in the U.S. Marshals. Sam had no delusions that their problems would magically disappear if Howard was behind bars or dead, but the difficulties would be greatly reduced as the Ravens' organization would probably fall apart without Howard—he was the key. "Talk to me, Molly. Did I say something that bothered you?"

Her shoulders slumped for a moment, but she shook her head. "No, it's just that I have to get back to work. We'll be fine."

Sam rose and crossed to her. She watched him, her eyes unreadable, but she broke contact and bit her lip. He reached out, touching a finger to her chin, and with a little pressure, urged her to raise her gaze to his. "Look, I understand that you don't want to have a relationship with me. I can't blame you, but don't put yourself and your daughter in jeopardy because of...of your dislike of me." He tried to stifle the hurt he felt that she didn't like him, but he nudged it aside. No matter what she felt for him, he couldn't let her go home and be in harm's way.

He had an idea and reached behind him, pulling the coffee table close so he could sit on it. "I can arrange for you to go somewhere else safe if I have to. I would rather you were here because nobody else knows Howard like I do, but I have a friend, Dave in the Bureau. He and his wife Cynthia live in Chicago, so it's not too far away. I know they would welcome you and Kelsie. It wouldn't be permanent, but just until things blow over."

"Oh, Sam…" Molly worked the hem again, watching her hands and not him. "It's not you, and believe me, Kelsie was foremost in my mind when I made my decision. I would like for Johnny to remain here though, if that's okay?" She finally looked at him again. "I'd feel better knowing he was safe with you until his problem is resolved."

He nodded. "Of course." At least she wasn't completely rejecting him. "I hope you'll re-think your decision though. I promise to keep my distance from you, if that's the issue."

A tear escaped from the corner of her eye and she dashed it away, shaking her head. "It isn't. It's a Friday anyway, so we might as well stay one more day, then go home on Sunday. It'll give Kelsie one more day on the beach."

Sighing, Sam stood. "Fine." He wandered into the kitchen, opened the fridge and stared into the interior for a minute before he remembered what he was looking for. A beer. He snagged one off the shelf and started to close the door, when Molly came up behind him.

"I'll have one too."

Sam shrugged and removed another, handing it to her. "Here."

She unscrewed the cap and took a long draught. Righting the bottle, she smiled. "Ah. That's good." With that, she turned and left the kitchen, pausing in the threshold, her eyebrow raised as she tipped her head towards the front of the house. "Want to join me on the porch? No talk of Johnny or the Ravens though. I just want to relax in the time we have left here."

Surprised, he hesitated; as much as he wanted to spend time with her, would it be wise? There wasn't much hope for them, but the night was perfect and they had been so comfortable for a few minutes out there before he had said something that had upset her. "Sure." He took another beer to save a trip back inside. He knew it still wouldn't be enough to numb his feelings, but it was a good start.

Instead of sharing the swing, they ambled around the side of the house to the beach. The moon was almost full and cast a silver path that danced across the lake.

Molly stopped and he caught his breath at how the moonlight seemed to kiss her face, highlighting her cheekbones and perfect skin. She had pulled a light long sleeved blouse over her t-shirt, and it fluttered in a faint breeze. She tilted the bottle and took a sip, letting her head fall back. "Look at the sky, Sam. All those stars! It's amazing!"

He tore his gaze from her, turning it heavenwards. It was gorgeous. Thousands of stars, like diamonds on velvet, dotted the sky. He glanced at her, enjoying her amazement as he took a swallow from his beer. "Beautiful." He looked at her rather than the sky, and she did a double take. He finally tore his eyes away and smiled. "Victoria's brother and I used to camp out here when we were kids. We would drag our sleeping bags out of the tent and lie on our backs looking for shooting stars. One time, we fell asleep like that, and it's kind of a good thing because we had brought a ton of junk food outside with us." He chuckled. "It was like we thought we were going to die of starvation in the 12 hours we'd be out here. We'd have bags of chips, soda, candy bars, cookies. You name it. Anyway, that night, we had gorged and came out to watch for shooting stars. It was a hot night and it was cooler than inside the tent. We woke up to snorting and scuffling, only to find a black bear in our tent ransacking our food."

Molly's teeth flashed as she grinned. "You're lucky it didn't attack you."

"Aw hell, with that much junk in her belly, she had no interest in two skinny boys, but we high-tailed it screaming our heads off back to the house."

Giggling, she slogged through the sand to the lounge chairs, and sat on the end of one, kicking off her sandals and digging her toes into the sand. "What did your folks say?"

Sam sat on the chair beside her own chair, and shrugged. "My dad said," Sam lowered his voice in an imitation of his father, "'Why the hell do you think I told you boys to eat in the house? So you wouldn't attract bears! Now the tent's ruined!'" He chuckled. "I had to work at a resort across the lake for the rest of the summer, gutting and cleaning fish for the vacationers in order to earn enough money to replace the tent. Worst job *ever*."

He finished his beer and set the bottle beneath the foot of the lounger, making a note to take it back to the house. "I got to be an expert at it though. I could clean a fish in about five minutes and earn five bucks doing it. It was just all those damn scales. And the smell..." Sam shuddered at the memory of the fishy smell. "One or two that I catch myself isn't a big deal, but dozens a week is something else entirely. No matter how many showers I took, the smell of fish lingered on me. I even caught a couple of cute girls making a face and wrinkling their noses at me when I walked past them. Talk about a blow to my adolescent ego."

Molly burst out laughing, curling forward with her hand to her mouth as if to stifle the sound but she lost that battle as a belly laugh escaped and she flopped back on the chair.

Watching her, Sam grinned and he couldn't remember the last time he had smiled so wide and that made his grin even stretch just a little more. "You're enjoying my sad tales of woe just a bit too much."

Propping herself on her elbows, she tried to catch her breath, but the pose made her shirt drop away from her body and her t-shirt pulled against her breasts. "I can assure you that you no longer smell like fish."

"Good to know." Sam chuckled, then cracked open the second beer he had brought with him. On one hand, he wanted to be out with her all night, but he didn't know if he could take being in her presence and not being able to take her in his arms. Maybe it was better to just go to bed. After a cold shower. A really long, really cold, shower. He guzzled half the beer.

* * *

Molly caught her breath, as she straightened to take the last drink from her beer. She wasn't much of a beer drinker, but it tasted good out here on the beach. The scent of the air, tinged with smoke from someone's bonfire, the mosquito spray she had used and the damp marshy smell of the lake and sand was like a balm, easing her stress. She glanced at Sam when he tilted his head back and downed the rest of the bottle. Why couldn't things be different? She had never felt this way for anyone before, and it figured the one man she fell for was the one she couldn't have. She tipped her beer, but lowered it in frustration when nothing came out. "Shoot."

Sam handed her the fresh one he'd just opened. "Share mine."

Their hands touched when she accepted it, and she watched as he followed her movements as she took a swig. A little beer escaped her mouth and trickled down her neck before she could stop it. Sam's gaze scorched a trail down her neck, his eyes fixed on the progress of the drop. She pretended not to notice and took another sip, this time letting some drip out intentionally.

It followed the path of the other drop down her neck and across her chest, but it didn't make it to safety beneath her t-shirt. Sam interrupted its path with a finger. He skimmed his finger back up, retracing the drop's path, before burying his hand in the thick hair at the nape of her neck, drawing her closer. Although his touch was light and encouraging, it was as if he had pulled her to him with superhuman strength, making her feel light as a feather as she melted against him, as he licked the beer off her throat.

"Sam..." she breathed. His lips were hot as his breath warmed her skin, and she shivered at the sensation. The instant she had let the beer trickle down her neck she knew she'd made up her mind. She let her head drop back, allowing him free access. His lips traveled up the column of her throat, kissing, licking and nibbling. His hand burned against her stomach, and when it slipped under the hem of her shirt, and skimmed up, she moaned and turned her face to his, seeking his lips.

He groaned as she captured his mouth, her tongue darting in his, flavored with the beer he'd just captured from her throat. The taste mingled with him, and she wanted more. When his hand found her breast, she couldn't stop the mewl of pleasure. Molly found the edge of his t-shirt, sliding her hands beneath, loving the feel of his skin, so warm and soft but stretched over rock hard muscles. The contrast was intoxicating.

"Molly?" Sam pulled away, his eyes reflected the moonlight and shone with questions.

She licked her lips and tucked a few wayward strands of hair out of her face. Her emotions warred. On one hand, she knew she was opening herself up to heartache. As soon as Sam found out who Kelsie's dad was, he'd want nothing to do with Molly. That knowledge, instead of discouraging her from wanting more, fueled her desires. This night would probably be the last chance she had to be with him. Her whole life, she had sacrificed for everyone else. She had been surrogate mother to Johnny, raised Kelsie alone, went to school, worked, and never once had she asked for anything in return. Howard had no role in their life, and maybe there was a slight chance that Sam would never find out that Howard had fathered Kelsie. But if he did find out, Molly wanted at least one more night to remember. Was that asking too much? One night of happiness?

"Let's go to your room, Sam." She thanked god she had put Kelsie to sleep in Sean's room. She had intended on sleeping on the narrow bed with her, knowing she couldn't sleep in Sam's bed and not want to be with him.

"I don't want you to regret this in the morning. I know you don't want Kelsie hurt, and I'll promise right now—I swear on all the stars in the heavens," he swept a hand towards the sky, "that I will never hurt her. I'd rather die than hurt her."

Searching his face, she saw only honesty and vulnerability. He was a man of his word. "I'm sure, Sam."

He pulled her close, burying his face against her throat. "I promise no matter what, Molly. Even if you change your mind right now and don't want to go to bed with me. Even if you end up hating me, I'll never hate Kelsie, because I think your daughter has already wrapped my heart around her little finger." He laughed against her skin, and Molly blinked back tears. Sam was making promises without knowing the full story. Would he be able to keep them?

"You're a good man, Sam."

He made a sound low in his throat. It could have been a groan or a growl, but when his whiskers scraped against her skin, she made her own indecipherable sound.

* * *

In a rush, they gathered their empty bottles and raced for the house, hastily brushing sand off their feet as they hit the porch.

The instant the door shut behind them, Sam drew Molly into his arms, wanting to slow down, but at the same time, he needed her right now. He kissed her softly, smiling against her mouth when her hand wrapped around his neck and she rose up, thwarting his efforts to savor the moment by branding his mouth with a fiery kiss.

"You're not going to let me take my time with this, are you?"

Molly gave a half moan, half chuckle. "Nope."

Eager to accommodate her desires, he reached for the hem of her shirt and pulled it up, breaking the kiss only when the material passed between them. She returned the favor, her hands scorching down his shoulders to his chest as she slid his shirt off him.

Never losing contact, they found the bed and took a brief moment to remove the rest of their clothes before lying down.

Molly lay on her side and her curves called to him.

Sam skimmed his hand down her ribs, to the indent of her waist and up to her hip. So soft and tempting. He found her mouth again, but lingered only briefly, as he swept her hair out of the way so he could find the silky, sensitive spot behind her ear. She shivered. Her breasts brushed his chest and it was all he could do to hold back, but her moan of pleasure made it worth the wait.

He kissed, tasted and teased his way down her throat, chest, abdomen and finally her most intimate places. Molly whimpered and clutched the back of his head, holding him even closer as her thighs clamped against his head. Unable to hold off any longer, Sam rose to his knees, holding her legs over his arms as he entered her with a groan. Her heat surrounded him, and he felt her muscles clench, drawing him in even further. All control vanished and he found her eyes as he sought his own release. Her lips were puffy from kissing, her hair tousled, and she held her arms over her head, bracing against the headboard. It was the sexiest thing he'd ever experienced. The sight of her tongue darting out to lick her lips sent him over the edge, and he threw his head back, tensing as wave after wave of ecstasy swept him.

* * *

Sam sat on the edge of the bed the next morning. He'd pulled a pair of khaki shorts on, but that was all. "We could be rushing into a relationship that neither of us is ready for—"

"But what if we end up throwing away something that could be good?" Molly felt a lump come to her throat. This wasn't going the way she wanted. After making love, she had lain awake fantasizing about a life with Sam. Why couldn't they could live right here? Her license was good in the whole state and she could transfer to a school in this part of the state.

There was still Sam's job, but maybe he could do something else. He seemed to love it up here and mentioned how he had felt disenchanted with his job even before Sean's death. The north woods would be good for him, and he said he had money put away so it wasn't like he had to decide on a job right away. She'd fallen asleep dreaming of the three of them living as a family. In the dream, Sam had never found out the truth of who was really Kelsie's father.

When she'd awakened and stretched, the glow from the dream still surrounded her, basking her in a blanket of peace and contentment, so when Sam rose from the bed and pulled on his shorts, she'd smiled and teased him about how he was going commando.

He'd looked at her blankly, then launched into the 'we're rushing things' speech. Somewhere deep down, she'd thought he would jump at her unspoken invitation to renew the relationship. Before he could answer her question, she rushed on, sitting up with the covers gathered beneath her chin. "The thing that scared me the most, was that the first time, we might have made love for the wrong reasons. I was there taking care of you. You might have confused gratitude for attraction." It embarrassed her to voice her fear, but she had to let him know. It wasn't like men typically drooled over her. Her hair was too curly and she was too short to be considered beautiful. "But last night—that felt real."

Sam's arm went around her shoulders, and she snuggled closer to him. His chest rumbled when he chuckled. "I can assure you, what I felt the first time was not gratitude. If that's all it was, I'd have sent you a basket of fruit or something. No, that night and last night was definitely pure attraction. What I was *going* to say before you cut me off was that I felt like I was dead for a year and suddenly, I'm alive again."

Her breath caught when his hand moved lower and stroked her upper arm. He turned her towards him and his eyes met hers. "Am I crazy?"

"If you are, then I am, too." Molly smiled and shook her head. "I'm scared to death though because Kelsie is getting attached to you. It's also something that never happened with the few men I've dated in the last couple of years."

"I'm getting pretty attached to her too, but it's her mother who's taking up residence in my heart." There was a smile in his voice.

She put her arm across his chest and lifted her face to him. He buried his free hand in the hair at the nape of her neck, and with the slightest pressure, angled her head. The faint light reflected in his eyes as his gaze danced between her eyes and her mouth. Anticipation built inside of her, becoming unbearable. His lips were only inches away.

He lowered his head, his mouth soft and warm against hers. She deepened the kiss, leaning into him. Their tongues met with a flash of heat, sending a tendril of fire through her veins. She ran her fingers up into his hair, then down to cup his jaw.

"Sam…"

Molly had no idea what she was pleading for, but it didn't matter because his mouth covered hers again as his hands roamed her body, pushing the covers out of the way. He pulled her onto his lap, turning her so he had full access. Wrapping an arm around his head, she bent, placing kisses along his jaw up to his ear. Encouraged at the low moan her kiss elicited, she ran her tongue along his ear, breathing lightly into it. A shudder swept him and she felt his excitement push against her thigh.

His voice was ragged as he said, "Molly?" He sought her gaze, but he still held her breast, his thumb brushing against her nipple distracting her from the question smoldering in his eyes. After a moment, he voiced it, "Do we have time before Kelsie's awake?"

Molly glanced towards the door. As if on cue, she heard a soft knock. "Mommy?"

"Apparently not." She sighed and stood, tugging the sheet with her, suddenly shy. "I'll be out in a minute, Kelsie."

Sam gently tugged the sheet from her hands. "Don't. You look beautiful." His arms circled her waist from behind, and a second later, his lips nuzzled the side of her neck. Her legs seemed to turn to liquid as she leaned back eyes closed, against the solid wall of his chest. "You're making this difficult."

He chuckled and nibbled her earlobe, whispering, "No, you're making this hard."

Her eyes flew open and she laughed, giving him a playful elbow in the ribs.

She caught his hand as he moved it up to her breast and laughed as she gave a gentle tug. "Come on. Time to make breakfast."

* * *

That night, Sam opened his arms in invitation as Molly returned from the bathroom and she was quick to snuggle into bed beside him. He loved the way she fit against him. Absently, he stroked her arm and she sighed, her breath fluttering over his chest.

He could get used to this. He'd never felt a connection to a woman like he did with Molly. They had already been through so much that it was hard to believe they had only known each other for a short while.

Everything between them felt right except for the timing. He still had a mission to carry out and she was leaving today. He had to avenge the deaths of his son and mother. Not just to keep his vow to himself, but to prevent the same tragedy from happening to someone else.

Molly turned over, her eyes searching his. "Why are you doing this, Sam? Why are you trying to protect my brother? You could walk away right now. I know you want to find the enforcer, but knowing what you want to do to him terrifies me."

Sam loosened his embrace and leaned away. It had always been his intention to kill the man. Whatever came after that hadn't concerned him. There was nothing left for him to care about and if he went to prison for murder, then so be it. He wasn't ready to give up on his plan to end the enforcer's miserable existence, but now as Molly watched him, her eyes wide with fear and Kelsie's tear-streaked face popped into his mind, he felt the first moment of doubt.

"I don't know. I have to think on it." It was the best he could do right now. For a year he'd been picturing every possible way of killing the monster who'd so casually given the order to torch Sam's mother's home, not caring about the lives of the innocent people inside. His only goal had been to send the strongest warning possible to keep Sam away.

"What about me? What about us?" The moon brightened the room and her eyes shone as they searched his face.

He knew what she was asking, but he couldn't give her an answer. Not now. He didn't even know where he was going to be tomorrow night, let alone next month or next year. "I don't know. Once this other stuff is settled, we can focus on what comes next."

Even in the dark, he saw the hurt in her eyes. He smoothed her hair back. "I can't believe I've only known you for a little over a week, but the one thing I'm certain of is that I care about you more than I've cared about any woman. It's all I can give you right now."

She nodded and inched closer. "I feel the same."

He tried to deny the joy that rose in him at her words, but his attempt was futile. The feeling stole into every nerve and muscle of his body, filling him with a warm glow.

A moment later, a cold wash of fear drenched him. Had he put Molly and Kelsie at risk by becoming involved with Molly? What if they were targeted like his mother and son had been? Before, he'd been worried because of her connection to Johnny, but what if they knew that she was here with him now? What if they found out about the relationship? He hadn't known they had broken his cover before, and it had cost his mother and son their lives. He had ridden all over the state looking for Howard, and it was almost certain that word had reached Howard. In fact, Sam had counted on it. He had hoped to draw Howard out of whatever hole he lived in.

Molly rose on one elbow, her other hand warm against his stomach. "What's wrong?"

He wanted to pretend everything was fine, but even without speaking, she must have sensed the change in him. Sam didn't want to cause fear, but he couldn't keep her in the dark—not when her child's life could be at stake.

"I think I made a big mistake. I should have thought it all through, especially since I've experienced it first-hand. It'll only make it harder on both of us."

She withdrew her hand, her eyes wide with shock. "What do you mean?" Her eyes narrowed as she tapped his chest. "You swore you'd never do anything to hurt us. What was that? Just a lie to get me into bed with you?"

Sam shook his head. "I'd never lie to you. I will admit to poor judgment though, in not thinking this through." He let his head fall back against the headboard with a thump. "There's more I have to tell you. After what happened to Sean, I vowed to get revenge on the Ravens' enforcer. I didn't expect to live through it, or if I did, I'd end up in prison. It didn't matter to me before."

"But it does now?"

"I want to make him pay. That desire will never go away, but I don't want to lose you in the process."

"So what are you going to do?"

"First I need to convince you to stay a few more days. I just want to be sure you're safe. Will you do that for me? I don't think Howard has connected me to this house, but the guys who followed us from your house are sure to have told Howard about you and that I was there too. He knows I'm looking for him, and that means, you're at risk too. It's like you have a double whammy hanging over your head. First, Johnny, then me. I'm terrified that Howard will try to get to me or Johnny through you and Kelsie. He's ruthless and he's already proven that he'll kill innocents to send a message. I was so hell-bent on getting Johnny away, and finding Howard, that I didn't stop to consider that he'll realize that he can send a message to both me and Johnny by hurting you and Kelsie." Sam closed his eyes and shook his head. How could he have been so stupid? His desire for vengeance had sapped his ability to think clearly. To think as he'd been trained to think.. "Will you give me a few more days?"

Molly tilted her head up to meet his eyes and he read fear in hers, but there was also something else lurking there. Guilt? He shook it off. It was his own guilt reflecting in her eyes. She finally nodded. "Yes. I want it over, too. I feel like our lives are on hold."

* * *

Sam held Molly the rest of the night and wished morning would never come. He had no choice. He had to go find the man who had killed his son, and in doing so would ensure Molly and her daughter's safety too.

Around two a.m., he heard a car pull in the driveway, and after a door slam, Johnny loudly thanked Victoria for the good time. Victoria's reply was inaudible, but she sounded annoyed. Sam grinned against Molly's curls. It took a lot to get Victoria in a bad mood. Johnny must have done something to really piss her off.

Johnny's curses were loud in the quiet house as he seemed to career down the hallway, bumping into the wall several times.

Worried about Kelsie waking up from the racket, Sam flung back the covers to go talk to him when the door to Johnny's room slammed, rattling the windows in the house. Molly started in her sleep, but didn't awaken. With an ear cocked towards Kelsie's room, Sam slid back into bed, but held his breath waiting to see if the noise had awakened the little girl. The house was silent, and Sam closed his eyes with a sigh.

In the morning, it took very little convincing to get Johnny to go. His eagerness surprised Sam, but he didn't dwell on it. He had too much on his mind. There was a lot to be done. Sam needed a new bike as his was back at Molly's and they couldn't leave Molly without a vehicle, so that meant finding one to buy. Sam knew a guy in the area who always seemed to have one for sale. He fixed bikes but sometimes the owners couldn't pay for the repairs or were only fixing them so they could be sold, so the guy had an ear to the ground about the best bikes for sale. By late afternoon, Sam had paid cash for a good used bike. He'd also secured enough cash to get Molly through a month if need be. He'd had the phone reconnected, since cell coverage was sparse. The next day, he took Molly and Kelsie shopping for items they hadn't brought with them and some extra clothes. He opened another bank account and transferred enough money to get them through several months.

If it hadn't been for the threat looming over them, the excursion would have been fun. Every minute he spent with them sealed them in his heart. His girls. Molly was the kind of mother he'd always wished Sean would have had.

More and more often, his thoughts of Sean brought a smile to his face instead of daggers of pain to his heart. If only they could live like this forever. He tried to fight his feelings. The timing was all wrong. Love was supposed to come when he was ready for it, not like a bolt from the blue.

Sam sat down to dinner, keenly aware that tomorrow night, he'd be in another town and already a sliver of pain stabbed at him. "This is great, Molly. I'm no good at cooking fish and this rice is fantastic."

Molly smiled and said, "You keep catching them, and I'll keep cooking them."

Sam grinned. He and Molly had taken Kelsie fishing and with all the chattering Kelsie did, he was shocked he'd caught anything, but the bass and walleye had been more than enough for a meal. "Deal."

"Why do you have to go, Mr. Sam? It's not going to be any fun here without you."

Molly's smile died and Sam felt a mouthful of rice stick in his throat. They had told the little girl that Sam and Johnny had to leave to take care of some business, but he had been unprepared for her tears. Even now, as another fat drop rolled down her cheek, he was torn between wanting to make her feel better or savoring thought that she'd miss him when he was gone.

"I don't want to leave, punkin', but I have a little job to do, and as soon as it's done, I'll be right back here."

Kelsie moped and poked her fork into her dinner. "I hate fish."

"That's not true, hon. You used to love fish." Molly smoothed Kelsie's hair off her forehead and said, "Try the rice. I think you'll like it."

He caught the worried glance from Molly, but could only shrug helplessly.

In bed that night, Sam held Molly, almost afraid to move for fear he'd forget the feel of her warm curves pressed against him. He kissed the top of her head.

"I don't understand why you have to find this enforcer guy, Sam. Why can't Johnny just move to another state or something?"

Sam sighed and tightened his arms in a gentle squeeze. "I wish it was that easy, but these gangs, they have connections all over the country. If Johnny surfaces somewhere, you can be damn sure that somebody is going to get the word back to the Ravens. The only possible way to get him in the clear is for us to find the enforcer, set him up and get him to admit to what he's done."

"Won't that get Johnny in trouble too?"

"I wish I could guarantee what kind of deal he'd get from the DA, but I can't. I can only speak up for him. My goal is for him to get off light with little or no time. Possibly one of those work release programs. He's managed to fly under the radar so far, which is a miracle that might work in his favor. Besides, it's not just Johnny he's after. By now, he'll know about me and you, or at least be pretty close to putting two and two together."

CHAPTER EIGHT

Molly waved as Sam and Johnny rode out of the driveway. Crossing her arms, she leaned against the pillar on the edge of the porch. Logically, she understood what Sam was trying to do, but it didn't make it any easier. She was worried for his safety and her brother's, but with a sigh, she pushed off the pillar. There wasn't anything she could do.

Sam had left her an ATM card and given her the PIN, so she had access to money. He said he had a few accounts and had transferred a sizeable amount to get her through a few months if she had to, but he had promised to be back well before then, probably in just a few days. She wandered through the house. Kelsie was still sleeping, so she went into Sam's room and made the bed, resisting the urge to pick up his pillow and hug it to her.

The house already seemed empty. Restless, she went to the kitchen and began cooking pancakes for Kelsie. She told herself that she didn't miss Sam already. It had only been a half-hour. It was just that the house was so quiet with just her and Kelsie in it, ignoring the fact that only she and Kelsie lived in her home and she should be used to it. She went to wake up her daughter hoping that once Kelsie filled the house with her chatter, everything would be fine.

The next few days, Molly spent the mornings with routine chores while Kelsie played with a few stuffed animals and Barbie dolls they had picked up on their shopping excursions with Sam. In the afternoon, they headed to the beach for a few hours of swimming and playing in the sand. Dinners were grilled chicken breasts, hamburgers or hot dogs.

By the fifth day, Mollie had to get out of the house and see other people. She loved Kelsie more than life itself, but she was going to go nuts if she had to play Barbies one more time. At home, Kelsie had her friends in the neighborhood or the TV, but Sam had discontinued cable television shortly after his son had died, since he hadn't intended on coming back. He had offered to get it re-installed, but Molly hadn't wanted him to go the trouble. Besides, it would do her and Kelsie good to get away from television for a while. There were loads of books in Sean's room that were the perfect reading level for Kelsie. In her mind's eye, she had pictured reading aloud to Kelsie every night before bedtime, but the reality was that Kelsie fell asleep before Molly could finish more than a few pages. All the swimming and playing outside wore her out, but that left Molly with long evenings with no one to talk to and no television to fill the silence.

Tonight was no different. The sun hadn't even fully set although it was after nine. Bored, she picked up the book she had been reading at the beach and made herself comfortable on the sofa. For a half hour, she tried to dive into the story, but instead of getting lost in the pages, she was lost in her thoughts. Sam was foremost. What was he doing? Was he okay? Wondering was torture, so to save herself from imagining what horrible things might be happening, she replayed every intimate moment she and Sam had shared.

A knock on the door made her jump to her feet, the book falling to the floor with a thump. She didn't know anyone here, but maybe it was a friend of Sam's. That was the most likely possibility, but there was also a remote chance it could be one of the Ravens. Unsure of what to do, she hesitated until she heard a familiar voice come through the door.

"Sam? It's me, Victoria."

Molly rolled her eyes and opened the door. "Hey, Victoria. Sam's not here right now. Is there something you need?"

The other woman frowned then shrugged. "Is Johnny here?" Her eyebrows rose in an expression of hope and Molly relaxed. So this was the real reason. "Sorry, he and Sam went out."

Victoria pouted. "Will they be back soon?"

"I'm not sure. They were taking a road trip on their motorcycles and playing it by ear. You know men. They don't plan anything."

"Oh. Well, I suppose that will be good for Sam with the year anniversary of little Sean's death coming up soon. Maybe he'll find some peace out on the road."

Surprised at the insight, Molly pushed the screen door open. "You're probably right. Would you like to come in? Maybe have a drink or something? I believe there's a bottle of wine in the fridge."

Victoria hesitated, then shrugged. "Sure. Why not? I don't have anything else to do."

Molly hid a smile. This was the Victoria she had first met. "Come on. I can rummage up a snack too."

After pouring them each a glass of wine, they took it out to the front deck along with a plate of fresh fruit and dip.

They sipped their drinks, quiet for several moments. Molly cast a sidelong look at Victoria. Had she and Sam ever been intimate? For some reason, she couldn't see the two together because Sam was such a quiet no nonsense kind of guy, while Victoria was loud and didn't seem to filter anything she said. Molly gave a mental shrug. Who was she to judge? It wasn't as if her track record with men was anything to brag about. On the other hand, she could totally see Johnny and Victoria as a couple.

Molly took a slice of apple and dunked it in the dip. "Did you and Johnny have a nice evening the other night?" She bit the slice, savoring the light creamy dip with its hints of black cherry and vanilla. Her brother had only mumbled something when she had asked him the same question, so now she was curious.

Victoria chuckled. "You mean he didn't tell you?"

Puzzled, Molly shrugged. "No, but then he doesn't normally tell me too much. Did something happen?"

"Johnny got wasted, which is fine—it's not like we're married or anything. We were having a good time and I was introducing him to some of the locals. He was playing pool with some of the guys."

"That doesn't sound so bad." Molly was relieved. She had expected something much worse.

"Wait, it gets better." Victoria paused to sip her wine. "Some rough looking men I don't know were playing pool at the other table, and before long, Johnny was challenging them to some games. Still nothing bad, but he was getting more and more drunk, and started talking—no, make that bragging— about getting shot at by some motorcycle gang. He made it sound like he fended off a whole posse single-handedly.

A jolt of fear stabbed through Molly's stomach. Johnny knew that he was supposed to keep everything quiet. She tried to act casual. "What did they say?"

"They laughed him off at first. I mean, no disrespect, but your brother doesn't exactly look like the tough guy he pretends to be." She threw Molly an apologetic look and continued, "I was laughing too, but then he mentioned Sam and how the two of them fought off some gang called the Ravens." Her tone became serious. "I saw some of the guys give each other a look like they knew something. It scared me, and I tried to get Johnny to shut up, but he just kept going on and on about this gang and how he and Sam were going to take them down."

Molly's heart had stopped beating somewhere around the time Victoria had mentioned the Ravens. What if those men knew one of the Ravens? What if word got back to the enforcer? Would they come looking for Johnny way up here? She set her wine down. "Did they say anything?"

"Hell yeah they did. They laughed, but it was the kind of laugh that makes you shiver, you know? Not the kind that makes you feel good. Anyway, Johnny said Sam had been shot so he'd had to save him. He even mentioned something about his sister patching Sam up."

"Oh God."

Victoria held the stem of the glass with one hand while tapping the rim idly with the thumb of the other. "I'm sorry. I finally got him away from the group by telling him it was time to go. I've been worried about it ever since." She shrugged as her mouth twisted into a wry smile. "I know you don't like me." She waved off Molly's instinctive protest and continued, "I don't blame you. I don't like you either."

Stunned at the candor, Molly could only gape at her guest.

"It's not personal, Molly. You seem nice enough, but I've loved Sam since he was a seventeen. He never noticed me though. I was just the kid sister of his best friend. By the time I was old enough where he might have paid attention to me, he was out of college and didn't come back here very often. Unlike Sam, I was stuck here year-round. I didn't get to leave when school started and go live someplace where shopping at the local "Fleet and Farm" isn't the highlight of the month."

Molly gazed at the lake as the last rays of the sun turned the water the color of fire. The eastern sky was a deep blue with the first few stars emerging to twinkle on the horizon. A loon's call echoed over the still water. "I can't imagine wanting to leave this place."

Victoria rolled her eyes. "Sure, it's pretty, but it's also boring as hell. I dreamed of moving to Chicago or New York." She toyed with the empty glass, and Molly thought about offering a refill, but since Victoria had already admitted to not liking her, all she wanted to do was get her out as fast as possible and call Sam on his cell. The other woman raised one shoulder in a careless half-shrug and said, "But, it wasn't meant to be. I got pregnant when I was nineteen and got married. I lost the baby a month later."

"I'm so sorry."

"Yeah, me too. If I had miscarried just a month earlier, I would have had my chance to pursue my dreams. Instead, I stayed here with Don. He had a good job at the sawmill, but we never got ahead." She glanced at Molly and must have read the horror on Molly's face at her callous recount of her miscarriage, because her eyes turned cold. "Don't judge me. I was devastated at the time, but it was years ago. I stayed married thinking we'd go off and have the whole dream of a little house and children, but Don liked to hang out at the bars more often than he liked to be home with me. I tried for years to make that dream a reality, but I ran out of energy. While I was working two full-time jobs to save money for our own house, he was out at the bars drinking up our savings. I finally had enough and kicked him to the curb."

Molly didn't know how to respond. She had her own rocky history with men and didn't consider herself even close to being an expert. "It sounds like you did the right thing."

"Yeah, well too little too late, as the saying goes. I'm pushing thirty and my dreams of being a model died a decade ago. When I heard Sam was back in town, I thought we'd finally have our chance, but instead, he had you and your little girl." She didn't sneer, but her tone came close.

Molly had heard enough of Victoria's sob story. She stood, picking up her own glass and taking Victoria's as well. "Look, you can say what you want about me, but don't use that tone in conjunction with my daughter ever again. Now, if you'll excuse me, I'm beat and was about to call it a night."

Victoria stood and took the last apple slice from the plate, and dipped it. "I don't know what tone you're talking about. I think your daughter is adorable." She popped the apple into her mouth.

Molly gave her a long look, but shrugged. "It doesn't matter. Thank you for telling me about my brother's encounter with those men. I'll call Sam and let him know."

* * *

"Sam?" Molly sat on the steps of the porch, wishing Sam was here. "Victoria stopped by last night and she had some news." She recounted her conversation with Victoria. "I'm worried."

"I'm not sure how much I trust Victoria's account of things, but I think we're about done down here. I got some info from an old contact that the Ravens haven't been around for a few weeks."

"So does that mean you're coming home?" She'd intended to say, 'coming back', but coming home had slipped out instead. This little cottage had become a home to her and already she hated the thought of leaving, but they couldn't stay here forever. She stood and leaned against the railing, craning to look around the corner to make sure Kelsie hadn't gone near the water. Molly was happy to see that she was still engrossed in some kind of Barbie drama with her new dolls.

Sam seemed not to have noticed her slip about home . "Yeah, I don't see any point in staying down here. The trail's gone cold."

She heard regret in his voice and it reminded her of Sam's personal mission in regards to The Ravens. If only he could achieve peace without seeking vengeance. Molly dipped her head, scuffing the toe of her tennis shoe at a dried chunk of mud on the porch, sending the small clump sailing off into the grass. "I hope Johnny's not causing too much trouble."

"No, he's doing okay. We picked up your mail and got the other things you asked for. If we get on the road in the next hour, we should be back by dinner time."

"I'll make something nice for dinner." As soon as she hung up, Molly spun in a circle, cheeks aching from the grin that couldn't seem to wipe away. Sam was coming home. It had only been a few days, but she felt like the time had crawled by.

* * *

Sam paced the living room. Since coming home the night before, he'd decided that maybe it would be a good idea to get his field office in the loop. He'd had no luck on his own at finding Howard. As much as it killed him, he might have to see if he could get any help, either officially, or perhaps from his friend, Dave.

If the Special Agent in Charge of the Chicago ATF office—Sam and Dave's boss—didn't agree, Sam would have to call the whole thing off. He had pleaded to go after the Ravens immediately after the funerals of his son and mother, but was denied. He requested again after seven months, but again, the SAC had refused. He said Sam was too close to the case, his grief still too acute. So, the bureau had plodded along with their investigation, but it was going nowhere. At least it seemed that way to Sam. While he wasn't able to participate, he saw the memos. The ATF's special arson lab had determined that the cause of the fire that took Sam's family was definitely arson, but that was as far as it got. They didn't have enough evidence as to who had started the fire and who had ordered it.

Sam rolled his shoulders, and tilted his head to work out a kink. He stalked to the window and stared at his dusty bike parked in the drive behind Molly's vehicle. He'd missed the bike. The one he'd picked up hadn't felt right to him and he'd let Johnny ride the new bike back. Johnny's bike now took up space in Tuck's garage. Johnny's motorcycle was too big of an identifier. Letting the drapes fall back together, he thought about why his mindset had changed. He no longer had a fatalistic frame of mind. He had a reason to continue living. The reason had curly dark hair and a smile that could light up even the darkest room. He smiled and sighed. Part of him worried his feelings were too intense too soon. Was this just a rebound of sorts? Was it just a way to avoid his grief by immersing himself in a relationship? When he thought of Molly and the sparkle in her eyes, he didn't think it was. It felt too real. They both had tried to deny their feelings and relationship, but he'd missed her the few days he'd been gone.

After crisscrossing the state of Wisconsin and hitting up their favorite hangouts that Sam recalled from his days in the motorcycle gang, they had come up empty. The only clue he really had was from Victoria, and that was far from concrete. Sam decided they needed more information, and the only place he thought he might get up-to-date intelligence was from the ATF.

* * *

"Dave…it's me," Sam said, as he paced the beach. He'd wanted privacy to make the call, and early morning, the lake was still and peaceful. Birds called out and soaring overhead was a bald eagle. Somewhere around the bend in the bay, a fishing boat droned, but the sound was distant. "I need some help."

"Sam! It's great to hear from you. How the hell are you?"

Sam smiled at Dave's enthusiasm. "I'm okay." And he realized as he said the words that he really was okay. Better than he had been in a long time.

"Where are you? I tried calling your apartment but the line was disconnected. I was thinking about putting out an APB on you." Although Dave sounded like he was joking, Sam heard the underlying concern.

"I went undercover—"

"Undercover? You mean you aren't on leave anymore?"

"Um, not exactly. I'm on leave, but I was doing my own little operation."

Dave sighed into the phone. "Sam…"

There it was again, the pity that Sam had come to detest. "No, it's okay, Dave. It's not what you think." Sam shrugged. "Well, it *kind* of is, but not exactly what you're thinking." He went on to explain about his encounter with the Ravens and saving Johnny's ass, along with their subsequent escape to Sam's cabin. When he got to the part about Molly, he tried to skim over it by just saying he had brought Johnny's sister and niece here too, and that it was necessary to keep them safe."

"I don't have a good feeling about this, Sam. What can you possibly do on your own—legally that is?" Sam clenched his jaw. Dave probably guessed what the plan had been. Before he could answer, Dave continued, "Forget I asked that—I don't want to know."

"I'll admit that I can't guarantee that I'll play by the rules when I find him, but...but there are complications now. I don't want my actions to hurt anyone else." He drew in a deep breath and tried to sound nonchalant as he explained, "I have a good incentive to do things the right way."

There was a pause, and then Dave said, "Glad to hear it. You sound different, almost like your old self."

Sam lifted one shoulder as he bent his head and kicked at a water-logged stick on the edge of the beach. "Yeah, well, I feel more like myself, but don't get too happy yet. I want revenge on Howard still. That won't ever change and I won't stop until I get him—one way or another."

"I wish I had news on that front for you. You know they won't let me do much with the case either, since they consider me too close to it too."

"But you have more access than I do."

"That's true, and I'm sorry to admit that I haven't inquired lately. It's been tough going discussing the case like it's a routine case, when...when, damn it, Sam—I loved Sean too! And your mom was like a second grandmother to my kids." There was a catch in Dave's voice and Sam closed his eyes and sank onto his haunches, rubbing his forehead between his thumb and fingers. It had never occurred to him that the tragedy had affected his best friend. Since Sean's death, he'd cut Dave out of his life. It was too painful. Dave was like the brother Sam had never had, and he couldn't count the number of holidays he had celebrated with Dave's family. Sean had once even asked if Dave's kids were his cousins.

"I'm sorry, Dave. I...didn't think about how all of this affected you, Cynthia and the kids. I should have. I miss you guys."

Dave cleared his throat, the sound loud in Sam's ear. "No apologies necessary and you should know that. We miss you, too. The kids ask about their Uncle Sam all the time."

Dave's kids had called him Uncle Sam one time in all innocence, not knowing the patriotic image the name inspired, and after it was explained, they had used the moniker whenever they saw him. Sam chuckled. "Yeah, well tell them I hope to see them soon. Maybe you all can come up here for a weekend or something when all of this is over."

"Sam, I hate to say it, but what if it's never over? What if you can't do whatever it is you want to do with Howard? *We* know Howard ordered the hit, but the guy who gave that information is dead. Without something else to go on, even if you find Howard, there's not enough evidence to convict him. You'd need to get a confession or something, and good luck with that."

"The informant is dead?" Sam grabbed another stick and stabbed it into the sand, gouging out a hole, his mind racing. How could he arrest Howard now? He had only reluctantly considered arresting the man, wanting instead to mete out his own brand of justice, but now even arrest was off the table. Sam straightened and flung the stick into the gentle waves."

"Yeah, he was killed in prison awaiting trial on another case."

"Damn it." Sam drew in a deep breath. "Well, I'm not sure what I'll do now, but I'll figure something out. I'll try to play by the rules, but at the moment, I'm stuck anyway. I've been canvassing the state looking for the man, but haven't had any luck. If you hear of anything, will you let me know?"

"I will. Let me jot down this number you're calling from. It must be new because I don't recognize it."

"It's a pay as you go phone."

"I figured. I'll do a little digging on my end and let you know where the investigation stands."

"I appreciate that, Dave."

* * *

Sam paid for the groceries and headed across the street to the bakery after depositing his bags in the car. He hadn't told Molly yet, but he was thinking of taking another few days to head to the western part of the state. There were plenty of bikers there, too. It was the region of the state he hadn't yet canvassed. When he'd been with the Ravens while undercover, they had never spent time in that part of the state, so he had concentrated his efforts in the central and eastern regions instead. He wanted to make sure there was plenty to eat at the cabin, and to soften the blow—for Kelsie anyway—he made a detour to the bakery. Fresh donuts might deflect the little girl's wrath. Midweek, the bakery wasn't too busy. Good thing it wasn't Saturday or he'd have no chance of getting a good selection in the middle of the morning.

There were a few customers in line ahead of him and he used the time to make some doughnut selections. A couple of chocolate, a raspberry-filled, an éclair, and two with pink frosting and colorful sprinkles. He smiled as he imagined Kelsie's face when she saw them. He just hoped neither of the customers before him would choose them as they were the last ones in the case. Sam took a deep breath, inhaling the delicious aroma of fried dough, chocolate, vanilla, and coffee. They should bottle the scent of bakery. Not only did it smell amazing, but it brought back so many wonderful memories. This was the same bakery he'd been coming to since he was a child and not much had changed. Dark wood cases with glass fronts held a selection of cookies, cupcakes, pies and decorated layer cakes.

As he studied the coffee cakes, a flyer taped to the front of the glass caught his attention. The colorful poster showed a motorcycle and heralded a coming rally in the next town over. It boasted food and music along with vendors selling all kinds of classic bikes on display. Sam read the date. It was this weekend. It was bound to attract a ton of bikers. Maybe even Howard. From his undercover days, before Sean had died, Sam had attended rallies as part of the gang. While most who attended were just weekend bike enthusiasts, there were always some less savory characters who attended as well. He'd hated that while he was deep undercover, he had to act like the other members of the gang. The regular folks usually avoided Howard's group as gang members swaggered around the rallies. People would pass them, their eyes never quite meeting any of the bikers, as if hoping to not call attention to themselves. It worked for the most part, as Howard had no interest in people who weren't looking for what he had to sell.

This rally appeared to be one of the bigger events in the region, and he had a feeling it would attract the Ravens. It would be well attended, but the town wasn't near a big city, so police presence would be light. Sure, there would be hired security, but they never posed much of a problem.

Sam's turn came and he placed his order; his anticipation for seeing Kelsie's face dampened as his quest for revenge resurfaced. At least there was a chance that he wouldn't have to leave town to find the enforcer. If his suspicions were correct, the enforcer would practically waltz uninvited into Sam's turf, and like a wolf protecting his territory, Sam had no qualms about doing whatever it took to rid his world of the threat. Howard would pay his debt and now Sam had a collection date he could stamp on the bill.

CHAPTER NINE

As expected, Kelsie squealed when she saw the pink doughnut, and Sam pasted on a smile. It fooled the little girl, but Molly looked at him, one brow raised in question. "What's wrong, Sam?"

He shook his head. "Nothing. I just forgot to get the juice at the grocery store."

She looked doubtful, but accepted his lie. "Well, there's some iced tea. It might not go with doughnuts, but I can make up a pitcher for later this afternoon."

"That would be great." He smiled again, feeling like a louse for lying to her, but she couldn't know about the rally. If she found out, she'd worry that Howard would come for Johnny again. Sam worried about it too. Johnny had been making a name for himself at the local bars already, and people would remember him. Word got around in small towns and even though the rally was in the next town over, Sam was sure Johnny's reputation had already spread. Just the fact that he was hanging out with Victoria probably stirred gossip. Everyone knew she was newly divorced. The problem was, if Howard was going to look for Johnny, Sam had to make sure he didn't come anywhere near Molly and Kelsie. That meant Sam had to deliver him to Howard at the rally—give the gang leader no reason to look for Sam's cabin. Johnny would be bait and he wouldn't even realize it. Sam felt a stab of guilt at the cruel scheme, but it wasn't as if Johnny would stay away from the rally. He'd go with or without Sam so it was better that Sam would be there to cover his back.

"I'm going to go see about putting the boat in the water. I've been promising Kelsie for a few days, and I finally have it water-ready. We can go for a ride around the lake later, if you'd like."

Molly grinned. "Oh, that'd be wonderful!"

Sam grabbed an éclair and headed down to the dock. He'd readied the engine but hadn't started it yet. It had been over a year since he'd been on the water with it. He jumped in, and checked the engine as he mulled over the rally. The problem was how to keep the rally a secret from Molly? How was Sam going to explain his disappearance for an evening? He could say he was going to visit some old buddy or something. Maybe Victoria's brother, Tony.

That afternoon, Sam took Molly and Kelsie on a tour of the lake, all but killing the motor to go through a narrows into a back bay.

Molly's eyes shone as she looked around her, her arm draped around Kelsie who sat beside her. "Oh, Sam, it's beautiful!" She gasped and pointed. "Look, Kelsie, I think that's a beaver!"

Sam smiled. "Yeah, beavers like it back here."

Kelsie's eyes became huge as she watched the animal, only its head visible, swim thirty yards away. She turned to Sam, but only grinned before searching out the beaver again. She and Molly had a whispered conversation about it, and he thought it amusing that they whispered as though they were in church. Looking around at the still water, almost calm now that their waves had spread wide enough to dissipate, he decided it did seem natural to want to speak softly. Sound carried on the water and even normal voices sounded almost like shouting. Kelsie wore Sean's life jacket and when he'd catch a glimpse of her out of the corner of his eye, he could almost imagine it was Sean sitting in the boat with him. For just a few moments, he indulged in the fantasy, closing his eyes and letting it wash over him. And then Kelsie giggled and the fantasy ended. He blinked a few times, grateful for the sunglasses, cleared his throat and took a swig from his water bottle.

"This was always my favorite part of the lake. There aren't any homes on the shore, and it's so quiet. Sometimes I'd come out here to fish, and I'd feel like I was the only person for hundreds of miles. Water skiers don't come back here because it's not deep and hard to get into the bay, and most prefer to stick to the main part of the lake."

"Think I'd love to float out here with a good book to read and cold drink. It would be pure heaven."

"Well, next time, you can read while I fish."

"What about me?" Kelsie looked from Molly to Sam. "What can I do?"

Sam stood and moved over to the cooler they'd packed and offered Kelsie a pouch of fruit juice while he dug out another bottle of water. "I can teach you how to fish. Before you know it, you'll be a good little fisherman," Sam joked, then realized that he'd spoken as if there were going to be a next time—enough next times to teach her how to fish.

Molly must have come to the same conclusion because the smile dropped off her face. "Sam, I've been thinking. We haven't seen any of the people you're worried about." She spoke in vague terms for Kelsie's sake, but Sam knew she meant Ravens. "And I just think it would be okay for us to go back home now. My boss was okay with me taking emergency time off, but he's not going to go for me staying up here indefinitely. And I don't have that much vacation saved up anyway."

At her words, a wave of sadness crashed over Sam, catching him by surprise, and he sat on the seat opposite Molly and Kelsie. Of course, they couldn't stay here forever. Molly had a life to get back to. Sam sighed. He wished that things were different. He wished that he could teach Kelsie to fish. Most of all, he wished his son was in the boat with him, too. So many wishes, and none of them could ever come true.

* * *

Sam threw a light jacket on to conceal his shoulder holster, but felt almost naked without his leather jacket. He should have bought a new one. He hoped Molly wouldn't notice the firearm, but there was no help for it. No way was he going unarmed.

Johnny walked out of the spare room, twirling a key ring around one finger. "Hey, Sam. What's up?"

He canted his head towards the front of the cabin. "Can you step out on the porch with me? I have to ask you something." Sam checked to make sure Molly was still busy helping Kelsie with her bath. He'd made sure they spent most of the day at the beach. With any luck, they would both go to sleep early, and by the time they woke up, this whole thing would be over.

"So...what'd you wanna tell me?"

"We have someplace to go tonight."

"We do?"

"Yeah. We're heading over to the bike rally. It's over in Kendall."

Johnny grinned. "All right!"

Sam shook his head. "Quiet. I don't want your sister to know. We're not going to have a good time, we're going to find Howard, the enforcer in the Ravens."

The grin withered and his face blanched. "But...*why*? We haven't had any trouble since we left Molly's house."

"Exactly. Do you think you can stay here forever? You may not have much of a life, but Molly does. She has a job and she has classes in the fall. As much fun as this has been, it can't go on indefinitely, and the only way to make it safe for her to go home is to finish this. As long as the Ravens are hunting you down, she can't go home."

Johnny bit his lip. "I guess so, but if they're going to be at the rally, I can't go. If they see me, they'll kill me!"

"You have to go. You're the bait."

"No way! I...I can't. I can't do it."

Sam clenched his jaw and strode up to Johnny, grabbing a handful of his shirt as he jerked him close. "Listen, you damn coward. Your sister—hell—your precious niece—are in danger because of you. You led those assholes right to her door and now you have to fix it."

Johnny gulped, his Adam's apple bobbing. "I'm sorry about that. I wasn't thinking, but—"

"But nothing." Sam pushed Johnny against the wall, rattling the screen door beside him. He balled Johnny's shirt in one hand and jabbed a finger in Johnny's face, close enough to make the younger man flinch. "Listen up. You either play the bait, and have me covering your sorry ass, or I'll turn you over to Howard myself. Either way, it'll fix this. Your call."

He nodded. "Yeah. Okay. I'll do it."

"Good." Sam released him and stepped back, glancing into the cabin. He heard Kelsie singing in the bathroom. "Now, here's what we'll do..."

Just as Sam finished outlining his plan, Molly opened the door. "Hey guys. Why so serious?"

Sam smiled. "Nothing. I was just warning Johnny about Victoria, but he told me he's a big boy and doesn't need my advice."

Johnny nodded. "Yeah, I can handle her. In fact, I'm going out with her again tonight." He lifted his chin as though defying Sam's advice. At least the kid was playing along even though he was scared spitless.

"I see. This sounds like it's getting serious." Molly crossed her arms, her eyes dancing as she sent Sam an amused look.

Johnny shrugged. "Anyway, I'm gonna get going. Can I use your car, Molly?"

"I guess so, since you already have the keys." Molly laughed. "Have fun."

"I will. See you guys later." He jumped to the ground, ignoring the three steps, and Sam hoped he'd show up at their meeting spot.

After Johnny pulled out of the driveway, Sam turned to Molly. "I hate to leave you ladies alone tonight but my old buddy, Tony, called me. He's in town and heard I was here. He wanted to hang out tonight."

"Is that Victoria's brother?"

Sam nodded.

"Well of course you have to go. You certainly don't need to ask my permission." She said the right words, but Sam could see the disappointment in her eyes, and he couldn't help feeling a little bit of joy that she would be sad he wasn't going to be here tonight.

"Be sure to lock the doors. I may be gone all night—Tony's quite the party guy—so don't expect me until late, and maybe not until morning."

"Oh." This time, she made no attempt to hide her disappointment and it was clearly written on her face. "Okay. See you tomorrow."

Sam should have turned and left right then, but couldn't bear to see her walk away like that. "Molly, I'm sorry. If I could stay here with you, I would." He leaned in, cupping her cheek with one hand as he kissed her. She accepted it, but pulled away after a moment.

"I guess I'll see you tomorrow."

* * *

Molly shut and locked the door as Sam rode off. She scolded herself that she had no right to expect him to be with her every second. After all, what they had was temporary. They both knew that. Molly had to go back to work soon, and Sam was still intent on hunting down Howard. While she understood why Sam felt he needed to inflict vengeance on Howard, she was torn. As much as she agreed that Howard deserved everything he had coming, he was still Kelsie's father. There was a chance he'd change his ways, and someday when Kelsie was older, she might want to get to know him. People changed. She thought of the man Howard had become, and thought of him ordering the hit on Sam's son and mother, and shook her head. Could someone who did that ever change enough to matter? Probably not and he had to pay for his crime. On second thought, she hoped Sam did find him, but her biggest worry was that Sam would end up dead or in prison and Howard wasn't worth it.

"Mommy, where did Mr. Sam go?" Kelsie wore one of Sam's old t-shirts as a nightgown. It was huge on her and hung almost to the floor, but she looked adorable in it, and Molly scooped her up and blew raspberries in the crook of Kelsie's neck, much to the little girl's delight. The move didn't distract her though, and as soon as Molly set Kelsie back on her feet, she repeated her question.

"Well, tonight, Mr. Sam is going to meet up with an old friend of his."

"He's not going to be here to tuck me in?" Sam had stood in the doorway the last few nights while Molly read to Kelsie, and then her daughter had insisted that Sam give her a goodnight kiss, too. Molly had known Sam was both touched and torn at the request. It had to have triggered memories of his son.

After finally getting Kelsie settled down and sleeping, Molly plopped onto the couch. She didn't feel like watching a movie and the selection was pretty much limited to Disney movies that she had already seen a dozen times each. She glanced at the bookcase beside the fireplace. It was well-stocked and she got up to peruse the titles.

It was a good mix of thrillers, historical, classics and, Molly giggled, romance novels. Somehow, she couldn't see Sam reading the bodice rippers. She sobered when she realized they probably had belonged to Sam's mother. Molly found a book that looked interesting and took it back to the couch. After an hour, she tossed it aside. It was okay, but she felt restless and couldn't concentrate. She was about to head to the kitchen to get a snack, when there was a knock on the door.

Molly froze for an instant then crept over to the fireplace and removed the poker from the bin of utensils. It was heavy, and was at least something to use as a weapon. She drew back the curtain of the window beside the door and let out a sigh of relief. It was just Victoria. She lowered the poker and unlocked the front door.

"Hello, Victoria." It suddenly occurred to Molly that if Victoria was here, where was Johnny?

"Molly. Can I come in for a second?"

"Sure." Molly held the door open for her, then closed it, locking it again. "What's up? I thought you were out with Johnny."

Victoria gave her a look of confusion. "Johnny? No. We didn't have plans tonight. Isn't he here?"

A sick feeling of dread coiled in Molly's stomach. "He told me he was going out with you."

"Dammit. I knew he'd go without me."

"Go where?"

"The Bike Rally over in Kendall. I called him a few hours ago and said I wanted him to take me, but he said no, he was beat and was just going to hang out here with you and Sam."

"Well, Sam isn't here. In fact, he's out with your brother."

Victoria put her hand to her forehead, and then drew it through her hair, shaking her head with apparent frustration. "My *brother*? He's not even in town." She crossed her arms, her lips thinning. "Molly, I think our men are up to something."

Our men? "Well, Sam's not exactly my man, but I think you're right. The guys lied to us about who they were going out with, but why?"

"I have no idea. If it was just Johnny, I'd chalk it up to him being a typical biker and out playing the field. A Bike Rally is a great place for a guy to pick up chicks." Victoria gave a sarcastic chuckle. "But I don't see Sam like that. You say you and Sam aren't together, but every signal I've seen you guys send to each other says differently."

Molly felt heat rush to her face and her first impulse was to deny it, but instead, she said, "Yes, I suppose all the signals are there, but it would never work."

Victoria looked confused. "Girl, if I had a guy like Sam looking at me like he looks at you, I would *make* it work."

Shrugging, Molly turned to go into the kitchen. "It's complicated. Come on in and have a seat." She motioned towards the table. "Want something to drink? We have beer, iced tea, and lemonade."

"See? You're already playing hostess in Sam's cabin."

"I'm not playing hostess. If Sam was here, he'd be the one offering, so I'm just doing what he would do."

"Whatever. I'll have a beer."

Molly took a beer, along with the pitcher of iced tea, and withdrew two glasses from the cabinet, adding ice to her own. "Here you go."

Victoria poured her beer, setting the bottle nearby. A small amount remained in the end, not quite filling the glass. She took a long swallow. "So, tell me what's so complicated about it? You're attracted to Sam, and he's attracted to you. It's a no brainer."

Molly wished she could tell someone, but she didn't know how much Victoria knew about Sean's death and it wasn't her place to talk about it. "Let's just say that there's someone in our history. If Sam knew about my background with this person, he'd hate me and worse, he'd hate Kelsie. I have to protect my daughter." She took a sip of the iced tea and it wasn't nearly strong enough to dull her emotions.

"Listen, Molly. I don't know you very well, but I've known Sam since I was a little girl." She gave a short, harsh chuckle. "Hell, I've been crushing on him the whole time, even when I was married to my sad sack of a husband. In all that time, I've never known him to be cruel to anyone, let alone a child. What kind of man do you think he is that he could hate a sweet little girl?" Victoria took another drink of her beer, but the look she gave Molly was filled with resentment.

Embarrassed, Molly glanced down, folding her arms and resting them on the table. "I didn't mean it as a slight to Sam. He's been wonderful to Kelsie. It's just, I wouldn't blame him for his feelings."

Victoria leaned forward. "Does this have something to do with Sean?"

Molly swirled her iced tea, the clink of ice cubes on the glass loud in the room. She didn't reply, just glanced up at Victoria and then gave a half-shrug.

"I have a confession to make."

Molly's head shot up. That was the last thing she expected the other woman to say. "Confession?"

"When Sean died, I thought *I* could be the one to comfort Sam. I was never in love with my husband, and started divorce proceedings when I heard about Sean's death." Victoria shook her head, her mouth twisted into a rueful smile. "It seems so cold-hearted now, but I wasn't thinking. I had this whole little fantasy about Sam needing me, but he wasn't around. I came back home because I had nowhere else to go. Then I heard Sam was back in town."

"And you thought that was your chance?" Molly felt fear, as cold as the ice swirling in her glass, grip her heart.

Victoria shrugged. "What do you think?" A smile tugged at the corner of her mouth. "But then I saw how he looked at you, and I literally wanted to claw your eyes out."

"Oh?" Molly sat up straight. When Victoria said confession, she really meant it.

"Yeah, but then I met Kelsie and Sam clearly adores her, too. I wanted to hate both of you, but I couldn't." Victoria poured the rest of her beer in the glass and downed it. "Besides, your brother is cute and he looks at me the way I looked at Sam."

Molly didn't know whether to be relieved that Victoria had given up her dreams of being with Sam, or worried that she was now interested in Johnny. While she hated to do it, feeling like she was betraying her brother, she had to be as honest as Victoria had been. "I love my brother, but he might not be the best guy to get mixed up with. He's had some problems of his own."

Victoria threw back her head and laughed. "Don't all men?"

"I suppose, but seriously, right now, Johnny has some motorcycle gang after him. It's why we came up here and how I met Sam. Johnny was already the target of a couple of attempts on his life, and in one of them, Sam saved Johnny, but was injured. Johnny and a couple of buddies brought Sam to me because Sam refused to go to the hospital."

"Oh, so that's what happened to his back."

"Yes, and he had to stay at my place a few days while he healed up. Then Johnny showed up with the Ravens hot on his tail and, well, it's a long story, but Sam brought us here thinking it would be safer."

"The Ravens?" Victoria had an odd expression on her face.

"Yes…why?"

"I saw some bikers wearing jackets that said that. They were in town earlier—probably going to that rally."

It felt as if every drop of blood drained out of Molly's head. "Are you sure?"

"Of course I'm sure."

"Oh no. You think the guys went to the rally?"

Victoria looked at Molly as if she was a simpleton. "Two guys—bikers no less — mysteriously lie about who they're with on the very same day that there's a big biker rally just a few miles away? I thought you were a smart lady."

Molly rubbed her temples. Sam wanted to kill Howard, and likely, the leader of the Ravens was here with his gang. "I have to stop Sam."

"Stop him? From doing what?"

"The leader of the Ravens was the one who ordered the torching of Sam's mother's house. He's the one responsible for Sean and Sam's mom's death."

"Oh crap."

"Exactly."

"Sam's going to kill that guy." Victoria shook her head. "What are you going to do?"

"Me?"

"Yeah, he's *your* guy."

Molly bit her lip. "He *can't* be my guy."

"Why not?"

Victoria had already confessed her feelings for Sam and had admitted that it was one-sided. That took a lot of guts, but could Molly trust her with this secret? No, she couldn't—not now and probably not ever, if she was honest. "He just can't. There are things about me that he doesn't know, and if he did, he would hate me." That was the gist of it. Victoria didn't need to know the details.

"Well, whatever you're hiding isn't gonna matter when Sam's arrested for murder."

Dipping her head, Molly massaged the back of her neck. "I know. I can't let that happen, and then there's Johnny. He might as well have a red bulls-eye painted on the back of his shirt."

"Maybe that's what Sam is counting on."

Molly looked up. "What do you mean?"

"Listen, I watch cop shows. Sam probably talked Johnny into being the little worm on the end of his hook."

"Sam wouldn't do that." But she remembered the hatred in his eyes when he spoke of Howard. He wasn't rational where Howard was concerned.

"Oh, I don't think he'd let anything happen to Johnny." She gave a dismissive wave of her hand. "My brother knew I liked Sam and would always tease me with news of his accomplishments. For instance, I know he's an expert marksmen. I don't know if that's what they call it, but he's a crack shot."

"I still can't let him kill Howard."

"The guy deserves it, but yeah, you're right. Sam would probably be charged with something."

"What if Howard's friends turn on Sam? It's not like Howard is there alone. Meanwhile, all Sam has is…*Johnny*."

"*Johnny!*"

They spoke in unison.

"Okay. I have to go find Sam and stop him." Molly jumped up, running to the door, but then jerked to a halt, slapping a hand to her forehead. "I can't do it."

"Why not?" Victoria had trailed her into the living room.

"One, because I can't just leave Kelsie alone, and two, I don't have a car. I let Johnny use mine."

Victoria fished in her purse and pulled out a set of keys. "Here. Take mine, and I can stay with Kelsie."

"Are you sure?"

Victoria shook her head. "I'd go myself, but..." She shrugged, her eyes moist as she confessed, "I don't think Sam would listen to me."

"Do you think he'll listen to me?" She prayed Sam would, but he had been focused on revenge for a year. Molly knew whatever she and Sam had going, it could never compete with a father's love for his son and his need for vengeance. She only hoped he'd listen to reason. It was a slim thread of hope, but it was all she had to cling to.

Victoria bit her lip, and nodded, swiping a finger beneath an eye. "Yeah, I do." She raised her chin. "Besides, it's about time I paid attention to some of the other guys out there who've been chasing me since I got back into town, including your brother."

Molly smiled. "I'm sure any man would be thrilled to have your attention."

Digging in her purse again, Victoria found a pen and scrap of paper, and jotted down her cellphone number. "And here. Call me when you get there and let me know what's happening. Do you know how to get to Kendall?"

Molly shook her head. "No."

"It's easy. Go into town and take the main highway straight west. It's the next village over; about ten miles. I'm sure you'll see lots of bikes on the way there."

True to Victoria's directions, the rally was easy to find. She just followed the stream of motorcycles and soon found herself in a small town not much different from Sam's town. Everywhere she looked were bikers riding all manner and style of motorcycles. She wished she'd paid more attention to what Sam's bike looked like, but she knew she'd never be able to pick it out among the hundreds. As she found a lot and paid to park, she realized it would be easier to find her own car here somewhere. It was pretty clever of Johnny to use her car instead of taking one of Sam's motorcycles. It kept the charade up that he was going out with Victoria.

Her car wasn't in this lot, and she crossed the street to another, but didn't have luck. Not that she knew what to do if she found it, unless Johnny was there. The noise of the crowd and the roaring of bikes cruising past made it difficult to think. Hold on a second, she could call Sam and see if she could hear anything in the background. Pulling out her phone, she tried to call him but it went straight to voice mail. Next she tried her brother, but couldn't reach him either. Exasperated, she shoved the phone in her pocket. Why did they bother carrying them if they weren't going to use them?

She wound through the crowd, wondering where she'd have the best chance of finding either Sam or her brother. Most of the activities seemed centered in a clearing just west of the quaint downtown area. White tents and vendors' booths dotted the expanse of open area and she headed for it. Bikes themselves were restricted to entering the grounds, probably due to the crowd, but people seemed to be happy to park on the street and mingle in the large field.

Molly made her way through the park searching for Johnny or Sam. While there was ample lighting, it was still shadowy and hard to make out anyone's face until she was close. It spooked her and she wished Sam had answered his phone. She wanted to ask around and see if anyone remembered them, but there was too great a chance that one of the Ravens might be about and she didn't want any of them to hear her. She moved through the crowd, and when she'd gone through the grounds once, she turned around and headed back, this time stopping at a few booths, once for an ice cream cone and then for a soft drink.

Each time, she had an opportunity to stand still and observe people chatting, drinking and generally carousing. For the most part, the atmosphere was easygoing and friendly, but there were pockets of bikers who remained apart, mingling only with each other. They looked harder and more dangerous. She decided it wasn't the number of tattoos on their skin, or even the amount of leather they wore, but instead, it was the lack of smile and warmth in their expressions. Howard had mastered that same look of cold amusement and she couldn't believe she had ever spent time with the man.

Molly tried to push the memories away, what little she had, that is. Ever since that rally seven years ago, any time she thought of it, she focused on Kelsie. She wouldn't undo the events of the rally if it meant that Kelsie wouldn't exist, but she wished with all her heart now, that some magic could change things and Sam could be Kelsie's father. Her daughter deserved someone like him.

She took a deep breath, struggling to squash the memories back into the mental box where she kept them under lock and key. Coming here had opened the box as if someone had taken a sledgehammer to it. If she closed her eyes, she could imagine being twenty-three again and excited to be around all the bikes and the tough guys. She'd attended that rally with a few friends, but at some point, their group had been separated. Later she found out they had gone for joyrides with a couple of bikers, but at the time, she'd wandered around looking for them, occasionally asking people if they'd seen the other girls. One inquiry had been to Howard's group. Molly remembered being a little tipsy at the time, but the guys had offered her a few more drinks. She should have said no, but she was flattered by the attention. The guys had been surprisingly polite, and when Howard had put an arm around her shoulders, she'd been nervous, but covered her anxiety with a laugh. She only vaguely remembered Howard trying to convince her to leave with him.

The next thing she recalled was hanging onto him as they raced along a two lane highway on his bike. He said something about taking her home, but the ride had taken a detour to some dingy motel that Molly could barely remember. She was foggy on the details and unable to recall if she had agreed to go with Howard, and that's what drove her crazy. The memory was hazy and she didn't know if she'd been given something in her drink or if she'd just drank more than she'd thought she had. Her next clear recollection was waking up at the hotel with Howard snoring beside her.

When she'd found out she was pregnant she didn't know what to do. Molly was young, but she wasn't so naïve that she expected Howard to marry her. She hadn't even planned on telling him, but he'd tracked her down months later, apparently having found out she was pregnant. Her cheeks burned at the remembered humiliation, just as they had that day. She took a sip of her soft drink. He'd looked at her big pregnant belly and then smirked at her. His only comment was he'd wanted to see if it was true. She never found out how he'd learned of the pregnancy. After that, she had never spoken to him again, but surprisingly, after Kelsie's birth, he had sent a few gifts, including what became Kelsie's favorite stuffed animal, Tiger. It was that act that had kept Molly from completely hating him.

Molly tore herself away from the past. What if she had missed Sam or Johnny because she had been lost in thought? She didn't think she had, but still, she had to pay attention. She turned, and stopped short. There he was. Not Johnny, or Sam, but like a ghost from the past and almost as if she had conjured him up with her thoughts, stood Ray Howard. The instant she saw him, he spotted her as well. At first, he squinted as if unsure, but then he smiled and ambled her way.

CHAPTER TEN

Sam kept in the shadows just outside of the beer tent. He sat on a barstool pulled up to a small high-topped round table. A dozen of them had been set up around the tent for those who wanted to drink outside. It was a make-shift beer garden, with strands of white lights strung between poles sunk into the earth. It formed an enclosed space, but still gave a view of the concourse. He had pulled his table a little deeper into the corner and had moved the other three stools that went with it to other tables. He didn't want anyone to join him, and the stools had quickly been claimed at the other tables so there weren't any extra anyway. The last thing he needed was some chatty motorcycle enthusiast striking up a conversation. If the Ravens were here, they would eventually make their way to the tent.

Johnny was inside and had called Sam, saying he'd already put down four glasses of beer. Sam gave a little shake of his head as he put his phone away after telling Johnny there was no sign of them yet. If Johnny drank any more he'd be too wasted to follow the plan. At the first sign of any of Ravens, Sam was going to call Johnny and warn him. Sam had instructed him to catch their attention, but then leave the tent. Hopefully, they'd follow him. Sam and Johnny had parked as close to the tent as they could, but they were still about a block away. Sam counted on the Ravens not wanting to do anything in public, but they would follow Johnny in hopes of catching him alone and away from the rally. However, he was only to leave the tent if Howard was in the group. It would do Sam no good if only the low level guys showed up.

Sam's role would depend on how the Ravens reacted. His darkest wish was that Howard would threaten Johnny, but only so Sam would have the law on his side when he killed the man. If Howard didn't make an attempt, then Johnny was supposed to act scared and beg that The Ravens spare him if he can give them an ATF agent. Sam would be that agent, of course. When Howard found out who Johnny was going to give them, chances were good he'd let Johnny go. Sam was worth more to them than the amount of drugs Johnny had lost, and besides, if he killed everyone who screwed up a drug run, nobody would risk it anymore. Failed smuggling attempts were a cost of doing business, and Howard should know that.

The hardest part would be how Johnny could explain how he knew Sam, and then Sam realized the truth was probably the best bet. They'd leave Molly out of it, just saying that Sam had saved Johnny's hide the last time. Johnny could just claim he was up visiting a girlfriend and had come to the rally and spotted Sam and talked to him for a few moments. Sam had rigged a campsite off an old fire road. It wasn't a legal campsite, but he figured the few hours he needed it, it would be safe from discovery. Police and forest rangers were too tied up with the rally to worry about one lone campsite.

When they showed up at an old forest road that led to a small pond where Sam had his campsite, he would be waiting. Sam would try to get a confession out of Howard first. The day before he had bought a pre-paid phone and had arranged for Dave, his partner from the ATF, to answer it and record the call. Since Sean's death, Sam had neglected his friendship with Dave. It had been too painful to hear Dave casually mention something one of his kids did in school, or something funny one of them did. Sam's face burned at the memory of his breakdown the night of Sean's funeral and how Cynthia, Dave's wife, had witnessed it. Had she told Dave about it? She probably had, not that his friend had ever mentioned it. Dave had just said that whenever Sam needed something, to let him know. Well, now he needed something, and Dave had been happy to help. Sam set aside his embarrassment and concentrated on the plans for Howard.

Sam had purchased a small camera usually called a nanny cam, the day before after taking a long drive to the closest electronics store. The camera was designed to be used to watch child-care givers, and Sam had it already rigged to the front of his tent. It was hidden inside a rolled sleeping bag that looked like it was just tossed on the ground. He'd wanted a live feed to Dave, but hadn't had time to get that set up. The phone recording would be good enough should something happen to Sam. The guy was a tech guru and would have no problem making that happen. With luck, they'd get it all recorded and no matter what happened after that, the recording would be safe.

Then Sam would attempt to arrest Howard while Dave stood by with Kendall's police on speed dial, ready to send back-up to Sam. The biggest worry for Sam was Johnny's safety. It was going to be tricky. Sam was counting on Howard forgetting about Johnny when confronted by Sam, and in the confusion, Johnny could fade into the woods. Sam had instructed him to only go about twenty feet in, and then lie flat. The woods were thick and pitch-black. Chances were good they'd never find him. He could always call the police later if he became lost. While it was remote out here, there were plenty of lake homes scattered in the woods. He'd run across one eventually.

With any luck at all, Sam's plan would work and Johnny wouldn't have to worry about the Ravens ever again as they would be locked up—at least the one who ran the show would be. Sam was confident the rest of the gang would break apart without Howard's leadership, plus once law enforcement dug into Howard's background, they were sure to find plenty to pin on the other members as well. With plea bargains to testify against Howard, there was no way any of them would ever ride together again. Sam took a deep breath and blew it out. The plan should work and soon Howard would either be dead or in jail.

Sam's phone rang and he saw it was Johnny. Damn that kid. It was already the third time he'd called.

"I don't think they're here, Sam."

Basically, Johnny was bored. Too damn bad. "Just sit tight. It's still pretty early." Sam glanced around, his gaze freezing on a woman with dark curly hair. No...it had to be a trick of the light. Molly was back at the cabin with Kelsie. "I gotta go, Johnny. I think I see something." He clicked off, and stood, ignoring the table as it wobbled. The woman stood with a drink in her hand and seemed to be searching for someone. Her back was to Sam, but the build and height were identical to Molly's. He started forward, intending to get a closer look and if it was her, to warn her away. As Sam shouldered through the crowd in the beer garden, a man from the other side of the concourse moved towards her. She backed up a few steps, and as the man came closer, Sam recognized him. *Howard.*

Sam quickened his step, all thoughts of the plan forgotten. His only thought was to get the woman who might be Molly, and get her away from the man. A group of five or six young guys entered the beer garden just as Sam was attempting to leave. He had to step aside and when he exited, Howard was only a few steps from the woman, and as he reached her, he threw an arm around her shoulders and drew her close. Although the woman stiffened, she didn't try to escape Howard's grasp. Instead, she shrugged at something Howard said to her. Then she did move away, but only a few steps. He couldn't hear the woman, but he could hear Howard booming voice as he asked, "So, how's my daughter?"

Then she turned in profile, and Sam staggered to a halt as his breath whooshed out as if he'd been sucker punched. *Molly? And Howard?*

* * *

Molly shrugged off Howard arm. He reeked of whiskey and body odor. "*Your* daughter? You've never even seen her."

"Oh, I've seen her. Cute little thing." Howard smirked. "She looks like a mini version of you." He plucked at one of Molly's curls and his touch made her shudder. "I see she still has that dog I sent as a gift when she was born."

His words raised goose bumps on her arms. The only time Tiger had been out of the house was the day Kelsie had taken the stuffed dog in for show and tell. The very same day Sam had first been in her home. Did he know about Sam, too? Why had Howard been watching her house? "She has no idea where the stuffed dog came from, so don't flatter yourself that she keeps it for sentimental reasons."

"But doesn't every little girl deserve to have a daddy?" His stench threatened to make her vomit as a breeze wafted it her way.

"Kelsie is a happy little girl and has other father-figures in her life. She certainly doesn't need you complicating matters."

"Oh? A father figure?" He threw his head back and laughed. "You mean your *brother*? That sorry excuse for a man?"

"You...you know my brother?" While Molly knew all about Johnny's relationship with the Ravens and presumably Howard, how did he know that Johnny was her brother? As far as she knew, there shouldn't have been a connection at all, especially since they didn't share the same last name and never had.

"You bet your ass I do. We have unfinished business, and a couple of my guys followed him right to your house."

"My house? You stay away from Kelsie. Please. I've never asked anything of you. All I want is to be left alone."

"I might be persuaded to stay out of her life if you tell me where your brother is hiding." He gripped Molly's arm, his fingers digging into the flesh on the inside of her bicep. She winced and tried to jerk her arm out of his grasp. "Once he returns what he has of mine, I'll forget all about Kelsie. Is he up here with you? This is a little outta your neck of the woods—whatchya doin' up here? Looking for another biker to make a baby with?" He released Molly with a sneering laugh. "Maybe we should try our luck again? After all, we made such a pretty one the first time and had fun doing it."

"You know, I don't remember a thing about sleeping with you so it couldn't have been all that fun. I guess you could say you certainly didn't rock my world." Not only did she want to deflect the conversation from Kelsie, but she hoped it would distract him from asking about Johnny anymore. "Now, if you'll excuse me, I see my group up there and I have to catch up." She didn't wait for his reply, but just rushed towards a group of women who seemed to be heading for the porta-potties. She mingled with the group, and then joined another small group as they headed back down the concourse. Molly couldn't see Howard anywhere, and decided she must have lost him.

Now she really had to find Sam and Johnny and warn them about Howard. She had hoped Victoria had been wrong about seeing the bikers in town, but that hope had been put to rest.

* * *

Sam's first instinct was to storm the twenty feet between him and Molly and ask her what the hell was going on, but his law enforcement training kicked in. Choking back his anger and hurt, he ducked back into the beer garden and watched between the strands of lights. He slid his phone out and called Johnny, warning him about Howard. As he put his phone back in his pocket, Howard grabbed Molly's arm and despite Sam's anger, he moved towards the entrance once again. No way he could stand by and watch Molly get manhandled and do nothing about it, but before he could get through the crowd, Molly had pulled free and taken off at a brisk pace and he lost her in the crowd.

Torn between wanting to follow her and completing his mission, Sam hesitated. So many questions coursed through his mind. Had Howard been serious when he'd made the comment about Kelsie being his daughter? If it was true, how could Molly keep that from him? He didn't have time to spend thinking about it any longer as Howard entered the beer garden. He scanned the crowd but didn't seem to know anyone. Sam wondered where his biker friends were. Surely he hadn't come to the rally by himself? Sam tugged his ball cap lower. He didn't think Howard would recognize him since the last time they had seen each other, but he didn't want to take a chance. Not yet. He needed to get him alone first.

Howard entered the tent and Sam hoped Johnny followed the plan. Sam peeked inside the tent and saw Howard approach Johnny. Backing away, Johnny's face twisted with fear. It was no act. *Shit.* Sam edged into the tent and took a place at a table behind and to the left of Howard. He tried to catch Johnny's eye and let him know he was there, but the kid's eyes were glued to Howard.

Straining to hear their conversation, Sam caught a few words here and there. Howard was asking if Johnny had what he owed him. Johnny shook his head, and held up his hands. What were they saying? Sam had to take a risk and get closer. There was another table beside Johnny's. Sam moved to it, keeping his back to Howard. He could hear them now.

"I don't care what sorry excuse you have. I want my money or the product." Howard's voice was just as evil and gravelly as Sam remembered.

"The mule was caught. What was I supposed to do?"

Howard snorted and said, "You should have done a better job of arranging the shipment."

"I'm sorry I suck at this, but it's not like I had a choice." Johnny sounded so pathetic, Sam almost felt sorry for him. "I didn't exactly volunteer. You said my sister would have an accident if I didn't follow your directions."

Sam had to fight the urge to glance back. The bastard made the young inexperienced guys do the dirty work, so if they were caught, Howard's hands were clean. There was no paper trail to him and so far, he'd been able to evade all charges. Maybe there was a chance they could work out some kind of deal for Johnny.

"You were the new guy. Think of it as initiation. It's what we do."

"I just wanted to ride my bike." Johnny sounded lost and forlorn.

Sam shook his head and sighed.

"Speaking of your sister, guess who I ran into outside?".

Sam didn't hear Johnny reply, but Howard said, "Your sister."

"Molly? No, she's back home. Besides, she wouldn't be caught dead at a bike rally. She hates bikers."

Howard roared with laughter; the sound tearing through Sam. "That's not how I remember it. Did you know me and

Molly go back a ways? Like...let's see...how old is your little niece?"

"What?" Johnny sounded confused and Sam wished he could turn and watch his face. Did he know anything about Molly and Howard?

"Your niece. She must be about six by now."

"What are you talking about?"

"Shit, I knew you weren't too bright, but I thought you could do simple math."

Johnny backed away from the table, and Sam turned his head as Johnny came into view. He looked as if he might vomit any second and Sam empathized.

Johnny pointed at Howard. "Kelsie? *You're* Kelsie's *father*?"

Sam had to see Howard's face when he replied. He had to know for sure. Shifting, he brought the man into the edge of his vision.

Howard spread his hands, his smile wide as if he was a proud papa. "The one and only."

Sam balled his fists on top of the table, imagining burying one and then the other in Howard's face.

"You're a lying son of a bitch—" Johnny charged the table, the action ripping Sam away from his morbid fantasy. Sam pivoted, arms stretched wide to stop Johnny. Howard would kill him and be able to claim self-defense. "Johnny! No!" Sam wrapped his arms around Johnny, struggling to hold the angry young man.

"Hey, don't believe me, just ask your sister. There she is now."

Sam whipped around to see Molly rushing towards her brother. She ignored Sam and grabbed her Johnny's arm, trying to tug him away. "Listen to me, Johnny. Whatever he told you— it's not like he said."

"You mean what he said is true?"

Molly glanced at Howard, her gaze snagging on Sam for a moment before shifting back to Johnny. "It's true he's Kelsie's father, but we never had a relationship. I met him at a bike rally, had a few drinks, and the next thing I remember is waking up at a hotel with him. It's not something I like to talk about."

It sounded as if Molly had been drugged--raped. It made sense, but was it true? Why hadn't she told him when he had first mentioned Howard? Sam didn't have time to think about it as Johnny's face darkened and he lunged at Howard again. Sam took the brunt of the force against his chest as he blocked

Johnny. Ignoring Sam, Johnny pointed at Howard over Sam's shoulder and shouted, "You threatened to kill my family, and all along, you knew Kelsie was your own *daughter*? What kind of sick asshole are you?"

He elbowed Sam in the side of the head in his attempt to get to Howard. Sam reeled, staggering to the side. He reached out and grabbed Johnny's sleeve. Part of him wanted to release the kid and let him do what Sam had longed to do for a year, but it was one thing to kill Sean's murderer and something totally different to kill Kelsie's father.

Howard grabbed the front of Johnny's shirt, balling it in a fist and pulled him close. "I'm the asshole who's going to end your life." He yanked a gun from the back of his waistband and shoved it against Johnny's stomach. "

Sam swore and released Johnny to pull his own weapon, ramming it against Howard temple. His finger itched to pull the trigger. Nobody would blame him. Howard had made the first move and Johnny's life was in danger, but Molly watched, her face contorted in fear, her eyes wide in horror as they

darted between the gun against her brother's stomach, and the one Sam held. "Don't do it, Howard. Drop the gun."

"Who the hell are you? This ain't none of your business."

"Well, seeing as I'm an ATF agent, I can't very well stand by and let you kill this guy in cold blood now, can I?"

Howard couldn't turn his head because of the gun, but he tried to look at Sam out of the corner of his eye. "Hey, I know you. You look different, Brennan, but your voice is the same. You couldn't stop me before and I doubt you have the balls to stop me now. By the way, how's your family doing?" He slanted a smirk at Sam.

Caught in a stalemate, Sam clenched his jaw and vowed not to let Howard goad him into making a mistake. He couldn't be sure that even if he pulled the trigger and killed Howard, that Howard's finger wouldn't reflexively squeeze the trigger and fire into Johnny.

"Ray, please drop the gun. Why kill my brother? He's your daughter's uncle. If you care about her at all, you'll drop the gun."

Johnny's head moved a fraction as he caught his sister's eye. "Molly...don't. Kelsie would be better off with him behind bars for killing me."

Johnny was willing to sacrifice himself for his niece and Sam swallowed hard. He'd judged the kid wrong all along. "Do as your brother says, Molly." Sam had an idea but if it went bad, he didn't want Molly anywhere nearby. Molly crossed her arms, visibly fighting to hide her fear and terror. "No, I can't do that. I have to stay to make sure you don't all kill each other."

"Aw, there's my girl, looking out for me," Howard said, a grin stretching across his face.

Molly took a step closer to Howard. "I don't give a rat's ass about you. You raped me, but the last laugh is mine as I have the most precious daughter in the world, and she doesn't need you in her life. I'm pleading because I don't want my brother to die and I don't want Sam to kill you because I know he would regret it. It won't bring his son back and it would just tear him to pieces."

"How the hell do you know about Brennan and his kid?" Howard attention wavered, and Sam took advantage of the moment. Keeping the gun pressed against Howard temple, he twisted suddenly and grabbed Howard's gun hand, shoving it down as he brought his own body between Howard and Johnny and yelling, "Get Molly out of here!" Johnny spun out of the way and snatched Molly's arm, jerking her out of Sam's line of sight.

Sam's right hand slid with his momentum, losing contact with Howard's skull, but he maintained his grip on Howard's gun hand. Howard jerked his arm up despite Sam's attempt, and pulled the trigger. Sam felt a hot burn against his left side, but didn't release Howard's arm. With a grunt, he put all his weight into forcing Howard's arm lower until the gun was aimed at the ground. Now all the way in front of Howard, Sam used Howard's own weight against him and jerked him forward, angling the gun to the side and praying that no one was behind him, either inside the tent or outside of it.

When Howard lost his grip on the weapon, he stumbled, and Sam stifled a groan as the other man fell against him. Sam tossed Howard's gun towards a now empty part of the tent, and then clutched Howard's shirt, forcing him down. "On your knees, you son of a bitch. *Now!*"

He shoved his weapon against Howard's forehead, pressing until the barrel dug into the other man's flesh. "You don't know how badly I want to kill you. How I've planned this moment in my head for the last year."

Sam's chest heaved as blood pounded through his head. This was it. In an instant, he could obtain his vengeance. Only a millimeter of skin and a quarter inch of bone separated his bullet from Howard's brain. He grimaced as he fought the urge to kill the other man.

For the first time, Howard looked afraid and he sank to his knees, his hands rising. "Listen, I didn't mean for your son to die. It was just supposed to be a warning. I swear to God."

Sam's finger twitched and he almost gave in to his desire to pull the trigger, but Kelsie's face popped into his mind. Such a sweet and gentle girl shouldn't have her father killed like a rabid dog even if he was one. Instead of pulling the trigger, Sam put his hand on top of Howard's head and pushed him face first into the dirt, then he rammed his knee into the small of Howard's back to keep him down.

Sam removed his wallet from his back pocket and flipped it open, revealing his badge to a security guard who approached. "I'm Sam Brennan, ATF"

The security guard scrutinized the badge, and then nodded. "What happened?"

"I'll explain in a second. First, I need your cuffs. "

The guard handed Sam the cuffs and turned to clear out the bystanders, asking those who had witnessed the event to stick around to be questioned, and sending the rest away. From his tone, Sam guessed he was an off-duty cop moonlighting as security. Sam snapped the cuffs around Howard's wrists. "You're a lucky man, Howard. You have the right to remain silent..."

* * *

"I'm going back in!" Molly tried to push past her brother, but he wouldn't let her past him.

Johnny put his hands on her shoulder. "Just wait a few minutes until we know it's safe."

"But I have to see if Sam's okay. There was a gunshot!"

"I know, I heard it, but he's fine. If he was shot, Howard would have run out here by now."

That made sense, but Molly bit her lip and tried to peer around him into the tent. A security guard had entered only a minute or so ago and now people were exiting. From the conversations she overheard she learned that Howard was the one on the ground. Had he been shot? On one hand, she was relieved it wasn't Sam, but she prayed for Sam's sake, he hadn't killed Ray Howard. More security swarmed the area and Molly heard sirens approaching.

A few moments later, the same security guard who had first entered stepped out, a hand-held radio held to his mouth. He was calling for medics to the tent.

Molly stepped forward. "I'm a paramedic."

The security guard looked her up and down. "You're a medic?"

"Yes." Molly fished into her purse and pulled out her work ID. "I'm not from this county, but I'm licensed for the state."

"Well, come on in and take a look."

At first, Molly headed for Howard, who stood between two security guards, his hands behind his back. When he saw Molly, he swore at her. She looked him over but didn't spot any injuries and asked one of the guards, "I'm a paramedic. What's the matter with him?"

The guard shook his head. "He's fine. The other guy over there needs some attention though." He pointed to the back of the tent. She looked in that direction and saw Sam sitting on the ground, his back against the front of the bar. His face was chalky and dotted with sweat as he held his side. His eyes appeared closed and a shard of fear pierced her heart. "Sam!" She rushed to his side. "Can you talk to me? Where are you hurt?" She put her hand on the arm he clutched to his side, gently pulling it away from his body.

Sam's eyes opened, and he tried to sit straighter, but winced at the effort. "Of course I can talk. It's nothing, just a little scratch."

"Let me be the judge of that."

"Molly, get away. You can't be here." He sounded weary.

Stung at his words, she pulled her hand back. "I'm sorry I didn't tell you about Ray Howard, but right now, I'm a paramedic who just wants to help you." She tried her best to sound professional and not like a woman whose heart had just been torn in half.

Sam shook his head. "I don't mean that. When the other paramedics get here, they're likely to see the other wounds I had and wonder about them. I don't want you being associated with me and getting in trouble. We can discuss the other thing later." He grimaced. "Besides, it is just a scratch. I think Johnny's elbow to my head inflicted more damage."

"Let me just look and see how bad the scratch is." She doubted it was just a scratch from size of the bloodstain she saw beneath the edge of his jacket.

"I swear, it's nothing. I'll get a few stitches and they'll send me home. I'm just a big baby about these things—you should know that by now." He licked his lips. "But why didn't you tell me about Howard?"

Molly looked over her shoulder as more security entered the tent. So far, they were leaving Sam alone, probably figuring she was taking care of him and they didn't want to interfere "I was afraid you'd hate me or even worse, hate Kelsie."

Sam's eyes searched her face. "I could never hate either of you. You should know that by now."

"It's just she loves you so much already and I wanted to protect her."

His expression softened and he blinked. "She loves me?"

"Of course she does. Why do you think she was acting so miserable the other day when she thought you were leaving?"

"I love her too, but what about her mother?"

Molly reached for his arm again. "Just let me look so the guards will think I'm actually doing something here."

He allowed her to see the wound, but when she tried to unbutton his shirt to get a better look, he covered her hand with his. "Wait—what about her mom?"

"Her mom?" His hand was covered in blood, but it didn't faze her. It was his question that made her pause. "Me?"

He nodded.

Molly took another peek around. Nobody was heading towards them yet, but sirens had stopped just outside the tent. "She loves you, too."

Sam grinned. "Today's my lucky day." He allowed Molly to look at his wound and he was right. It wasn't too bad. It was in an area that tended to bleed a lot, but wasn't life-threatening.

"I think you're getting delirious. Good thing the ambulance is here." Molly smiled. "I'll see you at the hospital."

Their brief moment of privacy ended as the ambulance crew swarmed the tent, and Molly stepped aside. Police arrived next and took a brief statement from Sam before he was loaded into the ambulance and taken to the hospital.

Molly wanted to follow it, but she and Johnny had to give their accounts of what had happened, since they were involved, and by the time they were cleared to leave, an hour had passed. Leaving the Sam's bike and Molly's car at the rally, Johnny drove Victoria's car as they headed to the hospital. Tomorrow they'd have to do a few trips to take all the vehicles home, but it was the least of her worries Her first worry was about Sam but he was probably going to be just fine. Her next worry was her brother. His whole demeanor seemed to have changed. Gone was his sulky little boy attitude and he was quiet as they drove. Molly glanced at him. "I guess it was a pretty big shock to you."

He shrugged. "Yeah it was. I never asked about Kelsie's father because I figured you were embarrassed he didn't come around, but I never thought something like that happened to you."

"You're right. I was embarrassed, and ashamed that I let myself get in that position, but over the last few years, I've come to realize it wasn't my fault. I was a victim because of Ray's actions, not my own. I was guilty of being young and trusting. That's it."

"I can't believe Howard killed Sam's son and here I was associating with the guy. It makes my skin crawl." Out of the corner of her eye, she saw her brother rub his arms as if something was actually crawling up them.

"He's a psychopath, but you aren't You are a good guy, Johnny. No matter how hard you try to be bad."

"No I'm not."

"I heard you when Ray had a gun against you. You were going to let him kill you to protect Kelsie."

Johnny cleared his throat but didn't say anything for a few moments, but then blurted out, "Sam's the good guy. He saved all of us. You should marry him."

Molly chuckled. "He hasn't asked me to marry him."

"He will." Suddenly he stiffened. "Where's Kelsie?"

"With Victoria. How else did you think I got her car?"

Relaxing, Johnny laughed. "I wasn't thinking. It's been a crazy night. I hope Victoria isn't too mad at me for not taking her tonight. She really wanted to go."

"I know, she came over and told me all about it. You know she really likes you."

"You think so?"

"I do." They made the rest of the trip in a comfortable silence.

* * *

At the hospital, when it became apparent that they were going to keep Sam until morning, Johnny took Victoria's car back home and promised to show up before noon to pick them up. He'd ride his bike to the rally site, get Molly's car and come back for them. It was like musical vehicles, but it would work out eventually.

Sam was already in a room sleeping, but when Molly explained the situation, the nurse allowed her to go in after checking Sam's chart and seeing her listed as a next of kin. That bit of information surprised her, and warmth spread through Molly. Next of kin? The nurse even gave her a blanket so she could cuddle up on the recliner. With all of the excitement, Molly thought she'd be too keyed up to sleep, but the next thing she knew, it was morning. A different nurse from last night had entered and was checking Sam's I.V. bag.

Molly glanced at Sam's sleeping form and asked the nurse, "How's he doing? It didn't look serious when it first happened." Had she missed something?

"He received a dozen stitches, but his blood pressure was a little low from blood loss so we had to give him some fluids to top him up. With it being so late already, it just made sense to admit him."

"Yes, I agree. Thanks." The nurse left and Molly stood by the bed and reached out to feel Sam's forehead. He still looked pale, but his skin was warm, not clammy as it had been in the tent. That was a good sign.

A moment later, the door opened again, and expecting the nurse, Molly turned to ask a question about antibiotics, but instead of the nurse, Johnny, Victoria and Kelsie entered the room. Kelsie grinned at Molly and was half-way across the room, arms wide, when she skidded to a halt, her eyes wide and focused on Sam.

"Mommy...what's wrong with Mr. Sam?" Even at her age, she realized that something was off.

"Shhh...hon. Sam has a owie, but he's going to be fine. They gave him some medicine so it wouldn't hurt anymore, but it made him sleepy."

Eyes still saucer-like, Kelsie edged past the bed as if afraid to come into contact with it. She wrapped her arms around Molly's waist and held on tight.

Smoothing back the curls, Molly bent and kissed Kelsie's forehead. "Don't worry, Kels. I promise you that Sam is going to be just fine."

Johnny glanced at Sam then to Molly. "So he's okay?"

"Yes, thankfully. He should be released after the doctor comes in to see him."

Victoria looped her arm in the crook of Johnny's arm and leaned against it. Her expression more serious than Molly had ever seen it. "You both could have died last night."

"We didn't though, thanks to Sam."

"Don't let him fool you, Victoria. Johnny was as much a hero as Sam. Did he tell you what he did?"

Victoria shook her head.

"Well, I'll tell you about it later. I think it might be too much for *someone* to hear." Molly nodded down at Kelsie, and pulled her close.

Victoria winked. "I look forward to hearing the story. Now, I think we should get going, Johnny. I'll drop you off so you can pick up Molly's car, then I suppose later, you'll have to go back and get Sam's motorcycle."

"Yeah. You want us to take Kelsie with us? She was upset when you weren't at the cabin this morning so we came here first, but I'm sure she'll be okay now, right Kelsie?"

Kelsie shook her head and clung to Molly. "I don't wanna go. I wanna stay with you and Mr. Sam."

Molly gave her a squeeze and nodded. "It's okay. She can stay." She looked at the bed as Sam stirred. "Sam will probably wake up soon."

At the mention of his name, his eyes fluttered open. "Hey."

Johnny waved as he and Victoria left. Molly reached out and brushed the back of her hand against Sam's cheek. "How are you feeling?"

"I feel great! They gave me something." He gave her a silly grin and she laughed. "C'mere." He reached for her but missed. "Hold still."

"I haven't moved."

"Oh. I must have."

Molly burst out laughing and Kelsie giggled.

"Hey! There's my girl!" He grinned at Kelsie and tried to sit up, but winced. "Ouch." He gave Kelsie a stern look. "Did you beat me up while I was sleeping?"

"No!" Kelsie's eyes danced. "Mommy said you have an owie again."

"I do, and I think your mommy should give it a kiss and make it all better, don't you?"

Kelsie nodded and giggled again, one hand covering her mouth.

Molly rolled her eyes, but smiled and smoothed the hair on Sam's forehead. "You need to go to sleep. The meds are making you goofy."

"Yeah, okay, but first I have to tell you somethin'." He motioned again, urging her to bring her head down as though he had a secret to whisper in her ear. Chuckling, she played along with him and put her ear near his mouth. His breath tickled when he said, "I forgot to tell you something back at the rally."

"What did you forget?"

"I forgot to tell you that I love you."

Molly pulled back. "What?" It must be the pain meds talking.

All traces of amusement had vanished from Sam's face. "I mean it. I know I'm drugged to the gills, but I was about to tell you in the tent, but everyone came in. I love you." He pointed at Kelsie. "And you, too!"

Molly and Kelsie exchanged a look and Molly melted at the joy on her daughter's face. Her own face felt like it was going to split, her smile was so wide.

Sam grinned. "I'm going to wait until tonight to officially propose so you'll believe me, but I want to marry you. We could live in the cabin. I've been thinking about it. I'll see if I can take on some assignment up here. There are plenty of meth labs and illegal weapons even up here. No shortage of work. I know it's asking a lot, but—"

Molly put her finger over his mouth. "Shhh…I believe you and I'm going to say yes, when you ask me." He tried to say something, but she bent to kiss him but pulled back, hesitant to kiss him with Kelsie right there. "Now go back to sleep so the meds will wear off, and you can get released."

"Mommy, can I use the bathroom?"

"Yes, of course. It's right there." Molly pointed to the door.

Finally alone, Molly leaned over and kissed Sam.

Sam returned the kiss, his hand tangling in her hair at the nape of her neck as he pulled her closer. "Mmm…how soon until I get out of here? I'd like to finish this kiss somewhere a little more private."

A thrill shot through her even as her cheeks warmed. "Soon. We have to wait for the doctor, but he should be in this morning."

Sam released her, settling back into the pillows. He blinked slowly, as if fighting sleep. "Maybe this is the drugs, but I was thinking, it's like, poetic justice or karma—something crazy like that."

"What is?"

"That Howard took my son, but I get to raise his daughter." His eyes brightened with moisture, but he smiled. "I think Sean would be happy about us. He would have loved Kelsie for a little sister."

A lump came to Molly's throat and she tried to blink back the tears. "Yes, it is poetic justice."

The End

If you have a moment, a review of this book would be greatly appreciated.

Other Books by M.P. McDonald

All books can be found on my website with worldwide links:

www.mpmcdonald.com

To learn about new releases, join my mailing list. Link also available on my website above.

Mark Taylor: Genesis (Prequel)
(This book is permanently free)

Mark Taylor's life changes forever when he finds an antique camera in an Afghan bazaar. Back home in Chicago, he discovers that the camera has a strange and unique ability--it produces photographs of tragedies yet to happen. Gifted with powers to change destiny, what drives him to risk his life for others? And when presented with photos of 9/11 a day before it happens, what else can he do but attempt to save lives and thwart catastrophe?

No Good Deed: Book One (A Kindle Top 20 Bestseller)

Mark Taylor discovers first hand that no good deed goes unpunished when the old camera he found during a freelance job in an Afghanistan bazaar gives him more than great photos. It triggers dreams of disasters. Tragedies that happen exactly as he envisions them. He learns that not only can he see the future, he can change it. Then the unthinkable happened and everyone ignored his frantic warnings. Thousands die. Suddenly, the Feds are pounding on his door and the name they have for Taylor isn't urban hero. It's enemy combatant. And, it means they can do anything they want to him. Anything at all.

March Into Hell: Book Two

Mark Taylor's life takes a dark turn when his heroism becomes the subject of a newspaper article. The media attention and a harrowing encounter while saving a young woman, puts him in the sights of the ruthless cult leader who covets the secret to Mark's power.

Uncomfortable in the public spotlight, Mark suspects he's being tested by the force behind the camera's prophetic magic. Battling his own self-doubt, he must maintain the secret or risk certain death.

Deeds of Mercy: Book Three

An unexpected visitor from Mark's past brings him unwanted attention from the authorities. Unable to decide who is friend and who is foe, Mark becomes a fugitive from the law, but with thousands of lives at stake, he is forced to put aside his fear of capture, and instead, seek help from his pursuers.

March Into Madness: Book Four

After thwarting a disaster in the nation's capital, Mark Taylor captures the attention of the CIA. Mark doesn't trust the agency—not with his history with them—but he agrees to demonstrate the miraculous camera in the hopes of creating a team to help him ward off future catastrophe.

Mark realizes too late that he should have listened to his gut instincts when he finds himself held in the bowels of DC against his will while agents of the CIA, intent upon learning the secrets of his psychic abilities, use him as a test subject.

* * *

Acknowledgements

This book would never have seen the light of day if not for the help and encouragement of Jessica Tate and Vickie Boehnlein. Jessica for being my writing buddy for so many years and pushing me with frequent writing sessions and instant feedback. Without her prodding me, I'd probably spend most of my time surfing the internet or watching television.

Vickie probably doesn't know it, but if not for her words of encouragement that evening at a mutual friend's house (Hi Lala!), I probably would never have finished this book. I had let it languish for so many years in order to write Mark Taylor books that I thought I'd never be able to finish this one, so thank you, Vickie!

In addition to Vickie poking me with a sharp stick to get this book done, she was also one of my amazing beta readers. Without them, I don't know what I would have done, so I'd like to thank them. My other beta readers were Win Johnson, Pam Moore, and Al Kunz. Thank you guys so much!

About the Author

My name is Mary McDonald and I've always been an avid reader since as long as I can remember. The day we got our first computer in the early 90s, I vowed I'd write a book one day. I started writing a few years later, and began sharing stories online in various writing forums. After about eight years of that, I finally had an idea for a novel, and that became No Good Deed.

I started writing under M.P. McDonald for my thriller series. You wouldn't imagine that this part of the book is always the hardest to write, and ironically, playing on Pandora right now is the song, *Who Am I*, from Les Mis. Fitting. Well, I'm not

24601, that's for sure. (Les Mis reference, sorry) In addition to being an author, I'm a respiratory therapist and have been working in that profession for twenty-eight years now. I can't believe it's been that long. A lot has changed in healthcare, some things good, some bad, but it never gets boring.

I live with my family in a small town in Wisconsin. We have a river a stone's throw away, and a lake just down the street. I recently got a fishing license and went fishing for the first time in years. I even baited the hook with worms and minnows. I only wimped out a little by wearing latex gloves. I've found at work at the hospital that I can pretty much touch anything gross as long as I'm wearing gloves. I even caught a fish the very first time out.